"Right now I can't remember a time when I spent a day with not a worry in the world," Slade said.

The weariness in his voice beckoned Elizabeth forward. "It's been a while for me, too." Even as a child she'd never felt totally free to be herself, to enjoy life without a concern. The thought made loneliness creep into her heart.

He rotated his chair around. His gaze snagged hers, intensity in his gray eyes, and something else—vulnerability—that reached out to her. Linking them. Her pulse reacted by speeding through her. She didn't want anything to happen to him or Abbey.

"I guess that's a price we pay when we grow up." He cocked a corner of his mouth in a half grin that faded almost instantly. "But my daughter shouldn't have to worry about it quite yet."

The appeal in those startling eyes, storm filled at the moment, touched a place in her heart that she kept firmly closed—had for years.

Books by Margaret Daley

Love Inspired Suspense

So Dark the Night
Vanished
Buried Secrets
Don't Look Back
Forsaken Canyon
What Sarah Saw
Poisoned Secrets
Cowboy Protector
††*Christmas Bodyguard*

††Guardians, Inc.

Love Inspired

*Gold in the Fire
*A Mother for Cindy
*Light in the Storm
The Cinderella Plan
*When Dreams Come True
*Tidings of Joy
**Once Upon a Family
**Heart of the Family
**Family Ever After
A Texas Thanksgiving
**Second Chance Family
**Together for the Holidays
†*Love Lessons*
†*Heart of a Cowboy*
†*A Daughter for Christmas*

*The Ladies of
  Sweetwater Lake
**Fostered by Love
†Helping Hands
  Homeschooling

MARGARET DALEY

feels she has been blessed. She has been married more than thirty years to her husband, Mike, whom she met in college. He is a terrific support and her best friend. They have one son, Shaun. Margaret has been writing for many years and loves to tell a story. When she was a little girl, she would play with her dolls and make up stories about their lives. Now she writes these stories down. She especially enjoys weaving stories about families and how faith in God can sustain a person when things get tough. When she isn't writing, she is fortunate to be a teacher for students with special needs. Margaret has taught for more than twenty years and loves working with her students. She has also been a Special Olympics coach and has participated in many sports with her students.

CHRISTMAS BODYGUARD

Margaret Daley

Steeple
Hill®

Published by Steeple Hill Books™

STEEPLE HILL BOOKS

Steeple
Hill®

Recycling programs
for this product may
not exist in your area.

ISBN-13: 978-0-373-67441-1

CHRISTMAS BODYGUARD

Copyright © 2010 by Margaret Daley

www.SteepleHill.com

Printed in U.S.A.

Then shalt thou call, and the Lord shall answer;
thou shalt cry, and He shall say: Here I am.
—*Isaiah* 58:9

To Marcella—thank you for all your support
through the years

ONE

"Watch out!" Slade Caulder said through clenched teeth, gripping the door handle on his SUV. Why had he allowed a sixteen-year-old with a permit to drive? Only a few more miles to the ranch—thankfully.

"Dad, I saw him coming out. I've got everything under control."

When he noticed Abbey sliding a glance toward him, his heart rate shot up even further. "Keep your eyes on the road."

"I'm gonna ask Gram to take me driving next time."

"No." Although he wished he could let his mother-in-law take over teaching his daughter to drive around Dallas, he wouldn't. It was his job.

The car gained speed. "Don't go over sixty."

"I'm not. I have to practice going highway speed. Quit worrying about me."

Yeah, sure. She might as well ask him to quit breathing. It wasn't going to happen. Abbey was all he had. At least this was an almost-deserted stretch of road.

Thud! Bam!

A blowout?

Suddenly the car swerved to the right toward the ditch along the highway. He lurched around and glimpsed the color leaching from Abbey's face. Her knuckles whitened as she fought the shimmying steering wheel.

"Daddy!" she screamed above the thumping sound followed by a whomp. "I can't control..."

"Take your foot off the gas. Put the brakes on. Get off the road." He schooled his voice into the calmest level he could manage. He desperately wanted to change places with his daughter, but knew he couldn't.

The rougher terrain along the shoulder alerted him right before the car plunged into the ditch, heading toward a tree growing in it. Slade twisted toward Abbey, but the seatbelt retracted, immobilizing him like a prisoner. The air bags exploded outward, slamming into him. His breath whooshed from his lungs.

Blackness swirled before him. He fought to stay conscious, but his eyelids slid closed as the darkness rushed at him...

Pain jolted Slade back from the void. He opened his eyes to a fine powder dancing in the air about him, choking him. He coughed but his body protested the sudden movement—a deep, throbbing ache spread out from his chest. As he raised his hand to his head, a hissing filled the air, vying with the sound of the engine running. Pushing the deflated air bag back, he tried to straighten but couldn't. The seat belt trapped him. His heartbeat thundered in his ears.

Suddenly, a thought drove the daze from his mind. "Abbey!" he called out, but she didn't answer.

Adrenaline pumped through him. He jerked his head toward his daughter. The action sent the world before him spinning and forced him to close his eyes for a few seconds. But the need to make sure his daughter was all right overrode everything. Alert, totally focused on Abbey, he squashed his own pain.

A tree limb, having smashed through her side window, pinned her against her seat. Her head tilted to the side, blood streaming down her face from multiple cuts. Panic battled to take over Slade. He tried to thrust the limb out the hole in the window so he could get to his daughter better. The branch refused to dislodge.

Think! He couldn't lose his daughter, too.

His hand shaking, he reached across and felt for her pulse at the side of her neck. Strong. But she hadn't moved. He quickly dug into his pocket for his cell and called 911. Once he knew help was on the way, he allowed a second of relief to flutter through him.

The vibration and sound of the motor grabbed his attention. He snaked his hand through the limb's small branches and managed to turn his SUV off. Then he rummaged in the compartment between the driver's seat and the front passenger seat for the first aid kit, tore into it and unwound some gauze. He needed to get closer to her to bandage her head. When he tried to unclasp his seatbelt, it wouldn't budge. Panic attacked him from all sides. He clawed at the strap as though he could pry loose the metal clamp that held him captive.

He looked over at his daughter, her eyes still closed, her blood soaking her. "I won't let anything happen to you," he whispered.

Taking in a deep breath, he composed himself. He couldn't lose control. Another fortifying gulp of air, then he pulled on the strap and finally disconnected it. Able to move more freely, he braced himself with one foot against the door and the other under the dashboard to compensate for the way the car leaned forward in the ditch. He angled toward his daughter and wrapped the gauze around the worst of her cuts to stem the blood flow. But when he drew his fingers away they were sticky and covered in Abbey's blood. The sight sent terror straight to his heart.

Abbey moaned and stirred. Her eyes popped

open, wide with fear as they linked with his. "Daddy?" She licked her lips, her face screwing up into a panicky look as her tongue ran over some blood. "I'm bleeding."

"Help is coming, honey."

He wanted to go around to her side to take a closer look at her injuries. When he shoved at the door, it creaked open, water gushing inside from the ditch. An earthy stench accosted him.

"Don't leave me, Daddy." Hysteria coated each word.

He twisted back toward his daughter, the cold water swirling about his feet. A shudder shivered up his body. "I won't." In the distance, the sound of the sirens blared. "It won't be long now," he said as calmly as possible, while inside the same helplessness he'd experienced when his wife had died five years ago washed over him. Suddenly, a sense of foreboding dominated all senses. Sweat popped out on his forehead. His hands shook.

Why did he feel like someone was watching?

Elizabeth Walker parked her red Trans Am in a space next to the Dallas office building where Guardians, Inc. was located. She'd hoped her boss, Kyra Morgan, wouldn't have anything for her yet. Although Elizabeth had been home almost a week since her last assignment, she could use another few days for rest and relaxation. Her last job in Phoenix had been a long one—ten weeks. But the call that morning asking her to come in to the office could only mean one thing.

She loved working as a bodyguard with the all-female agency, but some assignments required longer to bounce back from. The job demanded a lot of mental energy, and sometimes physical energy, too. The stress from always being on guard, always scanning the perimeter for trouble and never getting to enjoy the beauty of the moment heightened the importance of her downtime between missions. Kyra knew that well. So the fact that her boss called her in a little early meant this job was important—not something she would want to turn down.

Entering the suite on the second floor, Elizabeth greeted Kyra's secretary with a smile. "Is she in there?" Elizabeth tossed her head toward the closed door.

Carrie, her expression solemn, nodded. "She has a client with her, but she wanted you to go on in when you arrived."

"Who's the new client?"

"I gather someone Kyra knows."

That might explain why she was here earlier than usual after a taxing assignment. Her specialty was guarding children. She couldn't see Kyra turning down a friend, and from what her boss had said a couple of days ago, the other four employees who specialized in children were all still on assignments.

She pushed open the door to her employer's office and stepped into the room. A large man, over six feet, was pacing before Kyra's desk. As Elizabeth entered, he came to a stop and swiveled toward her. The most piercing gray gaze she'd ever seen homed in on her. For a second she glimpsed surprise in his expression from the slight widening of his eyes to the flare of his nostrils.

"This is Elizabeth Walker." Kyra came around from behind her desk and gestured toward a seating arrangement consisting of a couch and two wing chairs. "Elizabeth, this is Slade Caulder." Kyra, long legged and nearly six feet in height, moved toward the seats and took a chair.

Slade tipped his head toward Elizabeth and fit his tall frame into the other wing chair, leaving Elizabeth to take the couch. The intensity pouring off the man charged the air. The hair on her arms stood up.

Poised and professional, Kyra set a pad on her lap and wrote something down on it. "Slade has a problem that needs your expertise. His sixteen-year-old daughter has been threatened, and he needs the services of a bodyguard to protect her. I'll let him tell you what he's looking for."

His body held rigidly, he gripped the arms of the chair and turned his assessing gaze on her. Silence ruled for a long moment as Elizabeth felt catalogued and evaluated. A flicker in his eyes gave her the impression that she fell short. She lifted her chin a notch and focused her attention totally on him. Some people took her petite stature to mean she wasn't capable of defending someone. They were mistaken.

That sharp gaze switched to her employer. "Kyra, she can't be more than a few years or so out of high school herself. How can she guard my daughter effectively?"

Elizabeth stiffened and, before Kyra could answer said, "I'm flattered you think I look so young, but I'm nearly thirty." She bit back the words. "And I can show you my birth certificate if you need proof."

This time he didn't try to disguise his surprise as his look locked on hers.

"I assure you, Slade, Elizabeth is highly qualified and has been working for me for three years. She usually handles cases where a child is involved and has been successful in all her assignments. You wanted someone who could blend in with your daughter and her friends, especially at school. As you can see, she'll be able to."

"What kind of skills do you have?"

Elizabeth relaxed back on the couch, smoothing her straight black skirt as she crossed her legs. Slade's glance flicked to her four-inch heels, and she could imagine what he was thinking. She only indulged in wearing heels when she wasn't working and when she met prospective clients. It added to her height, giving the illusion she was taller than five feet three inches.

"I have a third-degree black belt in tae kwon do. I'm capable of shooting all kinds of guns, but my weapon of choice is a Glock Model 23. My last score on a PPC was 580 out of a possible 600."

"PPC?"

"Police Pistol Competition. I have taken down a man your size holding a gun on more than one occasion. Do you want me to show you how?"

One dark eyebrow rose. "I'll take your word for it."

"Why do you think your daughter is in danger?" Elizabeth kept her gaze glued to his, determined not to be the first one to look away.

"It started three days ago when we were in an accident. My daughter was driving when we had a blowout going sixty miles an hour. She's still learning to drive and couldn't handle the car. We ended up in a ditch. Next time I teach someone to drive, the first thing on my list will be what to do during a blowout."

Elizabeth sat forward, clasping her hands loosely together, and asked, "Someone caused your blowout?"

"I didn't know it at the time, but when my

mechanic was going over my car after the wreck, he discovered what he thought looked like a bullet hole by the whitewall. He notified the sheriff and me. Sheriff McCain agrees the blowout was caused by a bullet."

"Where was this wreck?"

"Not far from my ranch, near Silver Chase toward the end of Highway 156."

"Could it have been a hunter?" Elizabeth asked, although unease settled across her shoulders.

"At first I thought, maybe. None of us who live out that way allow hunting on our ranches but occasionally someone will try anyway. The sheriff told me it's hard to shoot a tire out. It would have to be either a lucky shot or someone very skilled."

"Like a sniper?"

He nodded.

The uneasy sensation spread down her spine. "What made you decide that it wasn't a hunter?"

Slade slanted his glance toward Kyra for a few seconds before returning the intense look to Elizabeth. The power behind his expression jiggled her nerves. This man was used to getting exactly what he wanted. Did he have a lot of enemies out there? Someone who would want to harm him through his child?

"This morning I went into my office. I hadn't been into work since the accident. Abbey had to stay overnight at the hospital for observation and had a rough day or two, but today she insisted on going back to school. I took her and went to work. In my mail, I received a photo of Abbey cut into pieces."

"Do you have it?"

"The police have it. I phoned Captain Ted Dickerson immediately after I informed the school of the threat. The principal called in extra guards until I could get something in place."

Kyra stood. "I want to contact Captain Dickerson and let him know you have hired us to watch Abbey." Her employer headed toward the exit and left Elizabeth alone with Slade.

"Where does Abbey go to school?" Elizabeth asked when the door clicked closed.

"Dawson Academy. It's a private school with more than adequate security. When I called, they said she was fine. After that, I came here. There's only so much the police or sheriff can do. I aim to protect my daughter no matter how much it costs."

"What kind of photo of her was destroyed? A school one? A recent one?"

Slade clamped his jaw together so tightly that a nerve twitched. "Recent. It was a picture of her cheering at a basketball game. The person who took it was probably only a couple of yards away." He leaned forward and his neutral expression became fierce, his eyes hard like smoky ice. "Which means the person was close to my daughter."

"While I can't prevent people from taking pictures, I can keep an eye out for anyone who is suspicious and stop them from gaining access to Abbey." She held his look. If someone wanted a person harmed, it was usually possible. But there were things that could be done to lessen the chance. She intended to take those precautions. "I am very good at my job. How will Abbey feel about having me follow her around?"

He blew a harsh breath out. "That's the problem. She's headstrong and independent. I think she would more likely accept you rather than a man guarding her, but I'm not going to kid you. She still won't like it, even though you're a woman and young-looking." His glance strayed over her, resting for a few extra seconds on her heels.

"Does she know she's in danger?"

"Until an hour ago I didn't know, myself. I haven't told her yet. I will this afternoon after school, when I introduce you."

"So what exactly do you want me to do?"

"Not let my daughter out of your sight. I want you to stay in the room next to hers at the ranch, escort her to school and back home until the person is caught." He plowed his hand through his medium-length black hair. "I'm curtailing her activities, which won't sit well with her, but with the security at Dawson Academy and you there, she'll be okay and more likely to accept the other restrictions."

"Who would have a grudge against your daughter?"

"I don't know. She's sixteen and popular at school. She's a cheerleader and has lots of friends."

"Have you considered that the person is really after you?"

That nerve in his jawline jerked again. "Yes. I think it's possible that someone wants to get to me through my daughter, and I'm looking into that. But first and foremost I have to know my daughter will be safe."

"That will be my top priority."

"It will be your *only* one."

His intense stare might have made a lesser person back off, but she'd learned painfully she had to stand her ground, especially in her profession. "You said you live on a ranch near Silver Chase. Which one?"

"The Rocking Horse, two miles before the end of the road on the left. Abbey gave it that name when we moved out there. She was five years old then." For just a split second a faraway look entered his eyes as though he was remembering how it had been when his daughter was five.

"What time do you want me at the ranch, Mr. Caulder?"

"Call me Slade. We'll be living in the same

house." When she nodded, he continued. "I'll pick Abbey up from school at three and be home by three forty-five. I'll let my mother-in-law know you'll be there by two. Mary can show you around before Abbey and I get there." He rose in one fluid motion.

She came to her feet, too. "One more question. How secure is your ranch?"

"Not very. It's a working ranch so people come and go. I have ten full-time cowhands. Jake Coleman, my foreman, has a house on my property, and five of the other men live in a bunkhouse near the barn. The rest live in town. They have all been with me for at least two years, and several of them are very good shots, but they would never hurt Abbey. More likely, they'd protect her with their skills. I have a fence around my property and a gate with a security code. There is a camera on the entrance at the gate, a security system in the home and some security lights around the property, motion sensitive." He paused, drew in a deep breath and added, "I'm having an expert look at it today. If it needs something more, then I'll get it. Whatever it takes."

Obviously money wasn't a problem for Mr. Slade Caulder. She'd heard the name before but couldn't place where. Maybe from the news. Or maybe Kyra mentioned him. But as soon as he left, she intended to find out more about her new client. It always paid to know as much as she could about who hired her—as well as any opponent she might be up against.

"I'll be there by two." Elizabeth held out her hand to shake his.

When his palm touched hers, warmth radiated up her arm. She nearly snatched her hand away. His firm grip indicated a self-assured man who liked to be in control. A man who wouldn't take no for an answer. An image of her father danced through her thoughts for a few seconds, driving all warmth from her. A quiver snaked down her spine, and she stepped back, pulling her hand away.

"Until then." His long strides ate up the distance to the door.

As he left the office, Kyra returned and made her way to her desk. "I'm sure you have a few questions."

"I've heard his name before. Who is he?"

"He's the founder of Digital Drive, Inc."

Elizabeth nodded. No wonder she recognized the name—his company was a huge, world-wide organization. "You seem to know him pretty well."

Kyra waved her hand toward the chair in front of her. "I knew Slade's wife years ago. She died five years ago, right about the time I left the Dallas police force. She had a long, hard battle with ovarian cancer. After she died, I kept in touch with Slade. A few times he has sent friends my way."

"Given his position, it's more likely he has the enemy, not his daughter."

"Probably. I've given him a few suggestions on how to protect himself. One being that he work from the ranch to minimize his exposure. Another being Joshua."

"For the security assessment?"

"Yes, but I also suggested Joshua guard Slade. You and Joshua would work well together."

"Uncle Joshua is the best."

"I know." Kyra's eyes twinkled. "I worked for him for many years."

Her uncle had been a police captain on the Dallas force until his retirement a year ago, at the age of fifty-five. He was the one who had recommended her to Kyra as a bodyguard. If it hadn't been for her uncle/mentor, she didn't know where she would be today. He'd helped her pick up the pieces of her life when she'd hit rock bottom five years ago after her husband left her for another woman.

"What kind of man is Slade Caulder?" Elizabeth finally asked when she found her employer staring at her with a question in her gaze. She didn't journey back into the past often. The memories hadn't been pleasant ones.

"He works too much, more so since Catherine died. He loved her very much, and I suspect it was his way of dealing with her death."

Avoidance? She'd become good at that, too. For

a moment she felt a connection to her client. "What about Abbey?"

"She's precocious. Looks just like her mother and has Catherine's soft heart. But you'll have your hands full keeping tabs on her."

"What kind of relationship does Abbey have with her father?"

"It used to be a close one when Catherine was alive, but I haven't been around them together much in the past few years. She's a teenager, not an easy time to curtail a person's life when they don't want much to do with adults."

"He mentioned his mother-in-law. Did he say her name is Mary? Does she live with them?"

"Yes, Mary Bradley. And yes, she came to help when Catherine was sick and stayed on after her daughter's death. Slade has mentioned to me how indebted he is to Mary for staying."

"What's she like?"

"Prim, proper, kind. I used to attend the same church as she did until she moved to the ranch. She is deeply faithful, like Catherine was."

Elizabeth was glad to hear that. It was Kyra and Joshua who had shown her the way of the Lord. Now she didn't know how she'd lived without her faith. But then, her first twenty-five years hadn't been what she called living. She'd just existed.

Elizabeth pushed to her feet. "I'd better head home and pack."

"As usual, call if you need any assistance. This assignment is special to me."

She smiled. "They all are to me."

An hour later, after contacting Joshua Walker, Slade sat at his desk at DDI, trying to clear it of everything of importance. He intended to work from home until this was resolved. Yes, he had a bodyguard for Abbey, but it was hard for him to turn something like his daughter's safety totally over to another. He needed to be around, to help protect her.

His secretary, Ramona, entered with a stack of folders and set them in front of him. "These are the files from personnel you requested. Anything else you want me to do?"

"I'll have a videoconference tomorrow at eleven o'clock with the department managers. Let them know. Also, scan the Wilson contracts when they come in and send them to me. I'll go over them from home."

"I'm taking my lunch break unless you want me to skip it and stay."

"No. Go. I'll be here when you get back. I'm not leaving until two-forty."

His secretary started to turn away but stopped. "If you need me to come to the ranch and work, I will."

"I might. Hopefully I won't be there long."

Once Ramona shut his door, Slade lounged back in his chair and swiveled it around to look at the tall buildings surrounding his headquarters in North Dallas. Ever since the wreck, his life had been whirling out of control. It was a lot like how he'd felt when Catherine died. He didn't want to go back to that time. He'd almost totally lost it. The only things that had kept him going ahead were his work and his daughter.

He shut his eyes, taking a few minutes to compose himself. The coming weeks would be hard, especially with the extra people in his house. They were only a few weeks from Christmas, which was supposed to be about family. Having strangers around would be awkward. He was a private person who didn't relish the intrusion.

A picture of the woman he'd hired to guard his daughter teased him. He still couldn't believe she was a bodyguard. The vision of long auburn hair hooked behind her ears, eyes the color of a pine forest, delicate features and a petite frame mocked that. She should be protected, not the other way around.

The ringing of his private line yanked him from his thoughts. He snapped his eyes open and snatched up the line, hoping it wasn't something wrong at the ranch.

"Slade here."

A long pause, then a mechanical-sounding voice came over the line. "Do you know where your daughter is?"

TWO

Slade clenched the receiver. "You'll regret ever having messed with me and my family."

Click.

His gut churned. *Leave my daughter alone. Come after me instead, coward.* The words—ones he'd wanted to tell the person on the other end of the line—shouted through his mind.

He slammed down the phone, then almost immediately grabbed it back up and punched the number for his security chief. After telling him about the call, Slade said, "See if that number can be traced. I need information. Now."

When he finished talking with him, Slade dialed the numbers for Dawson Academy. Four rings later—an eternity—a woman in the main office answered. "This is Slade Caulder. I need my daughter located and brought to the office. There has been another threat. I'm coming to pick her up."

"Yes, sir."

He surged to his feet as he replaced the receiver

in its cradle. Scooping up the files and some other papers he needed, he shoved them into his briefcase and strode toward the door. To keep his free hand from shaking, Slade squeezed it into a tight fist and stabbed the down button on the elevator with his knuckle. When he got his hands on the person behind this, he would regret ever threatening his daughter.

The scent of coffee wafted to Elizabeth as she entered her uncle's house, the place she called home when she stayed in Dallas. Bosco, her terrier mix, raced from the kitchen, jumping up on her, his tail wagging. His greeting never changed whether she was gone hours or weeks. She scooped him up and cradled him against her, barely able to confine his wiggling body.

Ah, it was good to be home—even if she was turning around and leaving today.

Again, she drew in the coffee aroma, savoring the smell that lured her toward the kitchen, where she knew Uncle Joshua always had a pot on the stove. Coffee was a mainstay for them both, especially when she was working. Right now, she needed a lot. Kyra had called her into the office before she'd had her usual four cups in the morning.

Uncle Joshua sat at the table with his mug and a Sudoku puzzle in front of him. He glanced up when she crossed to the coffeepot and poured herself some of the dark brew. "I was hoping I could talk to you before I had to leave, Beth."

Joshua was the only one who called her that. Every time she heard him say Beth she was reminded of how important she was to her uncle—and how important he was to her. He'd saved her life and pulled her back from the edge of despair. After her ex-husband had left, she'd had to grow up fast. And then when she'd been mugged, it had been a wake-up call, forcing her to see that she needed to take control of her life. Joshua had shown her how to do that. It was Joshua who showed her how to stand on her own two feet, and she hadn't depended on another person since then.

"I heard from Kyra you're working for Slade Caulder, too." After setting Bosco on the tile floor, Elizabeth poured some coffee in her mug and cradled it between her palms.

"Yeah, I just got off the phone with him about half an hour ago. I've agreed to be his bodyguard and do a security assessment. I'm due out at the ranch in an hour. He said his daughter might be in danger, too. Are you going to be her bodyguard?"

Elizabeth plopped into the chair across from her uncle and took a long sip of the hot drink while Bosco leaped into her lap and curled into a ball. "Yes. It looks like we'll be working together for the first time."

"Is that gonna bother you?" Her uncle's hazel eyes bore into her over the rim of his mug.

"No, why should it?"

He shrugged. "I thought my presence might make you nervous. If that's the case, I'll bow out and refer Mr. Caulder to someone else. It's not like I'm wanting for work."

Chuckling, she scratched her dog behind his ears. "You're busier now that you're retired than when you were a police captain."

He grinned. "Must be my charm."

"More like your connections and skills. If you can make Slade's house a fortress, it'll sure make my job easier. I'll feel like I'm on vacation."

"Already on first name basis with the man?" A gleam appeared in his eyes.

"The man asked me to call him Slade. That's all."

Her uncle held up his hand. "Hold on there, little one. You're mighty touchy this morning."

"One cup of coffee this morning wasn't enough."

"Oh, then that explains it, since it's almost noon. Drink up and I'll fix you a sandwich. I imagine you have to be at the ranch today, too."

"At two." She swallowed several more sips of the best coffee in Texas.

Joshua withdrew some turkey, Swiss cheese and lettuce from his refrigerator. "I think this will be a hard case. A ranch isn't the easiest place to secure, especially with people coming and going. That'll keep us on our toes. Might be a 24/7 job."

She grinned, giving him a wink. "I'm tough. I can take it."

Joshua studied her for a long moment. "Yes, you can now. You've come a long way."

"Thanks to you."

"That's what family is for, to help." Her uncle slapped together two turkey sandwiches.

"It is?"

His long strides covered the distance to the table quickly. He sat his large frame in the chair opposite hers and slid her plate across to her, then bowed his head and blessed the food.

His mouth twisted in a frown as he stared at her. "I should have realized Walt would mess up being a father. I should have been there for you." Elizabeth knew Joshua still felt guilty for the years of estrangement from his brother that had kept him from building a relationship with his niece sooner.

"You were when it meant the most to me." Elizabeth pinched off a small bite of turkey and gave it to Bosco before putting him on the floor.

"I have a lot to make up for."

"No, you don't. My dad was a lousy father, but I made it. I'm fine now. That's what counts." After another swallow of the caffeine-laden brew, she added, "I thought we decided long ago not to talk about the past. It's over with, and there's nothing we can do about it."

Joshua picked up his sandwich. "When you were in Phoenix, did you see him?"

"No. That's the way he wants it." *So did she.* Her father's dominance all through her childhood had smothered her. She'd never been able to please him, and he'd made it clear she was a disappointment to him. He'd put her down so much that when Bryan started doing the same thing, she'd struggled to retain a sense of herself.

"Ever since your mother died, Walt has gotten worse."

"I don't need my father. I don't need anyone."

"Everyone needs someone. God didn't make us to go through life alone." After taking a bite of his food, he washed it down with some coffee.

She wasn't really alone. She had Joshua and, more important, the Lord, because Joshua had led her to Him. Another thing she was grateful to her uncle for. "I'm starved. I missed your cooking when I was gone," she said, wanting to change the subject of conversation. Her father was in her past. She only looked forward now.

"I get the hint."

She savored her sandwich. The past ten weeks on assignment protecting a woman who was always on some weird diet had caused her to drop five pounds—five she didn't need to lose. She was glad her usual clients were children.

She'd nearly finished her lunch when her cell rang. Bosco barked at the sound, sitting nearby and staring at her bag. Leaping to her feet, she retrieved her phone and answered it.

"This is Slade. I'm heading to Dawson Academy because I received another threat to Abbey at the office. A call on my private line. The school just phoned to tell me that they can't locate Abbey. It's lunchtime, and the students are scattered all over campus outside. I know she could be there some-where, but I called Captain Dickerson to update him on the situation. He's sending someone to meet me at the school." Worry drenched his every word.

The beat of her heart slowed to a thud. "I'm not far away. I'll be there in fifteen minutes."

As she slipped the cell into her pocket, she picked up her purse and started toward the front of the house.

"What's wrong?" Joshua followed with her dog at his heels.

"Abbey's missing at school."

"I'd better come, too."

At the door she pivoted and petted Bosco good-bye. "No, get to the ranch and make it safe. I'm hoping it's nothing. It's lunchtime and a beautiful day. When I went to school, we spread out all over campus for lunch. I gather from what Slade said that Dawson Academy is the same way." She began to turn away but paused. "Oh, and will you pack a bag for me? Once we locate Abbey, I'll be glued to her like she's my new best friend."

"Will do."

Elizabeth hurried toward her car. *Lord, don't let anything happen to Slade's daughter. Please protect her.*

Slade pulled up to the school behind a patrol car and hopped out. He jogged to catch up with the two officers heading up the steps to the front entrance.

At the double doors into the school he said, "I'm Abbey Caulder's father, Slade Caulder. Thanks for coming."

"The captain filled us in on what has been going on with the threats," the older police officer said. "I'm Sergeant Gibson."

Slade entered the school behind the sergeant with the other policeman taking up the rear. After explaining who he was to the security guard and getting a laminated visitor badge, Slade quickly made his way toward the office to the right. The first thing he noticed when he came into the room was all the activity. The principal, Mr. Hartley, was on his cell, a frown on his face, nodding.

Slade headed for the man, whose expression indicated that Abbey hadn't been found yet. Slade's heart pounded so hard he felt breathless. When the man clicked off, he asked, "Have you found Abbey?" Fear caused a raspy edge in his voice.

The principal glanced at the officers, then directed his attention to Slade. "No. The security guards and some of the teachers are searching the grounds and having the students come inside early. They should be heading to their next class. The teachers have been informed and have returned to their classrooms."

"Have you made an announcement over the PA system?"

"No. Most of the students aren't in the building yet. They were spread out because of lunch."

Anger and frustration surged through Slade. He gritted his teeth and started to count to ten. He made it to three. "Make an announcement for Abbey to come to the office. Maybe she's in the building by now."

The man paled. "I'll do that, then make another one in five minutes." He moved toward the counter to the left.

"Slade, have they found Abbey?"

He spun around and saw Elizabeth threading her way toward him through the crowd in the office. The sight of her brought a momentary wave of relief. "No."

The announcement instructing Abbey Caulder

to report to the main office blasted through the building.

When Mr. Hartley returned, Slade said, "I would like to search, too, with Ms. Walker here." He gestured toward Elizabeth, who stood next to him.

"Fine. Our assistant principal can accompany you." Mr. Hartley waved toward a middle-aged woman who joined them. "Mr. Caulder and Ms. Walker will join the search for Abbey. Please accommodate them any way you can."

Sergeant Gibson stepped forward. "In the meantime, I want to talk to the head of your security, Abbey's last-hour teacher and any of her friends you can locate."

Slade followed the assistant principal out of the office, aware of Elizabeth a few feet behind him. If anything happened to Abbey… The thought chilled him. Exigency spurred him to quicken his pace as swarms of students began entering the building, jamming the hallway.

"Let's check her next class first," the assistant principal said and headed down a corridor to the left.

Slade scanned the faces of the kids. A sense of urgency charged the air. Slade kept surveying the people as he passed them. No Abbey. Each passing girl that wasn't his daughter made his heart pound a shade faster, hammering him with a fear he'd never experienced before: of losing his child. He forced air into his oxygen-starved lungs.

The assistant principal stopped at a classroom and spoke to a teacher standing at the door as students filed inside.

The instructor shook her head, then peered at him. "Abbey hasn't come inside yet. I've asked a few of her friends if they have seen her, and no one has."

"Thanks." He barely got the word out between parched lips.

Sweat beaded his brow. The press of people all around him prodded the fear forward to dominate all physical responses. He surveyed the students near him. His gaze latched on to Abbey's best friend zigzagging through the crowd.

"Lily, I need to talk to you," he shouted over the noise of the teens in the hallway.

The sixteen-year-old looked wide-eyed from him to Elizabeth, then to the assistant principal. "Mr. C, why are they looking for Abbey?"

"I came to pick up Abbey. Do you know where she is?"

Her eyebrows knitted together. "Is something wrong? The security guards are looking for her, and now we're having to come in early."

"She's needed at home right now." *And maybe for the rest of her life. I don't want to let her out of my sight.* His heart continued to throb against his chest.

"We were supposed to meet for lunch in our usual place, but she didn't show up. Has something happened at home?"

For a few seconds, words clogged his throat. He swallowed several times before he could speak again. "When was the last time you spoke with her?" he asked, ignoring Lily's question because he didn't really have a good answer.

"Right before our last class. I have algebra. She has English."

"Was she okay?"

"She didn't say anything, but I could tell she was tired."

"Thanks." He gave Lily a smile and began to turn away.

"Did something happen to Mrs. Bradley? Mr. C, what's going on?"

That was a good question—another one he didn't have an answer for. "Mrs. Bradley is fine. But I've decided that Abbey shouldn't have come back to school so soon after the accident."

He didn't give Lily a chance to ask any more questions. He dove through the mass of teens and approached Abbey's fourth-hour teacher. Taking a card out of his pocket, he scribbled down his cell number. "I'm going to keep looking for my daughter. If she shows up, please let me and the office know."

"Of course, Mr. Caulder. I hope everything is all right." The teacher's own apprehension seeped into her voice.

"So do I," he said, then turned toward the assistant principal. "Did anyone check with the school nurse? Maybe she wasn't feeling well. This was her first day back since the wreck."

"I'm sure the nurse heard the announcement and was alerted when the teachers were, but I'll call right now and check with her." The woman stepped away and took out her cell phone.

"If she isn't at the nurse's office, where else might she go?" The calmness that coated Elizabeth's voice spoke of a person who dealt in intense situations and kept her composure throughout.

He could use some of that calmness right now. He thought of all the times he should have spent with his daughter—not working to drive away the memories of Catherine's death. "Abbey is involved in cheerleading, basketball and drama."

"Why don't we check those places next?" Elizabeth asked as the assistant principal returned.

"Abbey isn't at the nurse's office."

Slade's gaze coupled with Elizabeth's. "Then let's go to the gym."

It took them ten minutes to scour the gym and locker rooms. No sign of Abbey. Slade left the gym complex, trying to hold on to hope that Abbey was all right, that somehow she hadn't heard the announcement. He clutched his cell as though having it in his hand would make it ring with news that his daughter was safe.

"Let's check the drama wing and then go back to Abbey's next class," Slade said to the assistant principal.

The woman escorted them down the long hall that led to the drama classroom and the area behind the stage. Most of the students were inside their classrooms by now, with only a few stragglers. Teachers were encouraging them to go to class immediately. Concern marked the faces of the people he passed.

Elizabeth fell into step beside him. Why didn't he get a bodyguard right after the wreck? Why did he think it was a hunter? If Abbey was kidnapped it would be his fault. How could he live with that? "If Abbey isn't here, I'm going to have the police bring in more officers. Nothing can happen to her."

"When we find her, I'll do my best to protect her." Although Elizabeth's words were spoken with a hard edge, her expression softened as she looked up at him.

A tough exterior meshed with a kind heart. He saw it in her eyes as he held the door to the drama room open for Elizabeth. She exuded confidence by the way she carried herself. To look at her a person would never think she was a bodyguard, and yet since he'd been around her, he'd gotten the distinct impression she could take care of herself in many tough situations.

Students were seated in the large drama classroom. The assistant principal walked over to the teacher to speak with her while Slade let his gaze travel around the room, fastening on each teenager there. Slade held his breath and finally released it in a rush when he saw the teacher frown and shake her head.

"She's not here," he murmured to Elizabeth, who scanned the area, checking out every nook and cranny. She shook her head at his words.

"We should still look everywhere. Backstage is a huge place—or at least, it was when I was in school."

"Backstage? Why would Abbey be there?"

"Does Abbey have a boyfriend?"

Slade went cold. "What are you implying?"

"She's a teenage girl. I have to think of all possibilities."

"No, she doesn't have a boyfriend that I know about." But what if she'd kept one secret? It wouldn't have been difficult to hide. The past few months he'd lived at the office, finalizing the unveiling of a new product. He should have been home discovering what was going on in his daughter's life.

"One of my jobs is to ask tough questions. Ones you might not want to hear."

The assistant principal approached. "She's not here. Let's go back to her fourth-hour class before we head to the office."

His gaze connected to Elizabeth's, Slade said, "First let's go backstage and make sure she isn't there."

"But she—"

The glare he sent the older woman halted her words. "Humor me."

"Fine." The assistant principal led the way through a long corridor that ran behind the stage and opened a door.

"What's back here?" Elizabeth asked as the woman switched on additional lights.

"There's a room where costumes are stored. Props and pieces of furniture are housed over there." The assistant principal flipped her hand to the right.

Some of the furniture overflowed the storage room and was stacked along the wall. "I'll look in there," Slade said.

"And I'll check the costume room." Elizabeth started toward the left.

"Dad, what are you doing here?"

Slade froze for a few seconds before he pivoted toward the voice. He closed the space between them in three long strides and clasped Abbey's arms.

Pulling her into his embrace, he hugged her tightly to him. She was okay.

"Dad, I can't breathe." Wiggling out of his arms, she backed away a few paces and tilted up her face to peer at him.

"Abbey, where have you been?"

Confusion marked her expression, but something more, too. Her brown eyes held a lackluster look. A pallid weariness highlighted her features. "I was tired. I thought a nap at lunch would help. I set my alarm on my watch to wake me before my next class."

"Why didn't you just come home? I'd have picked you up if you weren't feeling well."

"I didn't want to go home. I don't want to miss the last play practice before Thanksgiving weekend." She dropped her head. "And I wanted to see my friends. Go to the game tonight."

"We'll talk when we get home."

"Home? But I want to stay."

"That's not an option, Abbey. I came to school to get you. There are some things I must talk to you about." A conversation he didn't want to have at all and especially not in front of the assistant principal.

Abbey glanced at Elizabeth and frowned. "What's going on?"

"This isn't the place to discuss it."

"Is Gram all right?" His daughter's voice rose, fear pushing the confusion and exhaustion away.

"She's fine. Let's go to the office and check you out."

"I'll let everyone know Abbey has been found." The assistant principal withdrew her cell again and placed a call as they headed to the main office.

"Who is she?" Abbey asked, tossing her head toward Elizabeth.

"Abbey, this is Elizabeth Walker, a friend of Kyra Morgan."

Abbey's features pinched into a deeper frown as though that didn't explain anything. "Kyra? I haven't seen her in a while. Why—"

"Hon, I'll explain everything later. Let's go home."

Abbey came to a halt just outside the main office and faced him. "What's going on? Why are the police here?" She pointed at the two officers visible through the large plate-glass window, talking with the principal.

The ringing of his cell gave him an excuse not to answer. Instead, he faced the empty hallway they had just come down and answered the call from the ranch, glad for the interruption. "Slade here."

His housekeeper's frantic voice came over the connection loud and clear. "Mr. Caulder, there's been a break-in."

THREE

"What?" Slade hunched his shoulders and lowered his voice, keeping his back to his daughter. "A break-in?"

"I got home a few minutes ago from town and the front door was wide open. The alarm wasn't on. Mrs. Bradley is gone. Do you think anything happened to her?"

"Mary's at church. I called her there an hour ago. Is anything taken?"

"I don't know. I decided I'd better stay out on the porch until the sheriff comes. I phoned him and gave him the gate code." Hilda had dropped the level of her voice a few notches, but the frantic ring still sounded in her words.

"I'll be right home. Mary should be there before me. Don't go into the house." He snapped the phone closed and turned toward his daughter and Elizabeth.

"Is something wrong?" Abbey asked, her eyes narrowing.

"We need to get going. Do you have the books you need?"

"Dad—"

"We'll talk in the car on the way to the ranch. I promise."

"Fine. I've got everything I need." Abbey clutched the straps on her backpack and stalked toward the exit.

Elizabeth moved close, her scent of vanilla swirling about him. "What happened?"

"The house was open when Hilda, my housekeeper, came home from running errands."

"I understand your mother-in-law lives with you. Was she home?" Elizabeth started after his daughter.

"No. You've been doing your homework."

"I asked Kyra. I like to know everything I can going into a situation." She paused near his car and watched Abbey climb into the front passenger seat. "I'll follow you to the ranch."

He cracked a grin. "Are you sure you don't want to come with us?"

Although her expression was somber, a gleam lit her green eyes. "I'll be right behind you. You should be all right."

"It's obvious you don't know much about my daughter. I wouldn't be surprised if you hear her clear into your car when I tell her she has a bodyguard and why."

"Have fun."

The smile that graced her lips transformed her whole face. He watched her walk to her Trans Am and slip behind the steering wheel. When she waved at him, he suddenly realized he was staring at her. He quickly twisted toward his car door and wrenched it open.

The second he climbed into his Lexus, Abbey angled toward him. The corners of her mouth dipped in a frown. "What's going on?"

He switched on the engine and pulled away from the curb. Although the ranch was only half an hour away, it would be a *long* trip. "It began with the wreck."

She sat up straight, her eyes wide. "Am I in trouble? Am I getting a ticket?"

He shook his head. "I wish that were it."

"Dad, you're scaring me."

Good. She needed to be scared, so she'd follow the safety measures he was putting in place. But his daughter thought she was invincible, taking risks when she shouldn't. "Hon, there's no easy way to tell you this. Our car crash wasn't an accident. Someone shot the tire out, and that's why there was a blowout."

Abbey collapsed back against the seat. "What's that mean?"

"Someone has targeted—" he inhaled a stabilizing breath "—you."

"Me!" She flattened herself against the passenger door, totally facing him. "Why? What have I done?"

"I don't think you've done anything. I think they're angry with me and using you to get to me."

"Why? What have you done?"

A layer of sweat coated his palms, and one hand slipped down the steering wheel. He gripped it tighter. "I don't think I've done anything wrong, either." He wasn't even sure he was the real target, but he wasn't going to let his daughter think someone was angry enough with her to want to harm her. Not unless he was sure. Logically, he was the one the person was after.

"I don't understand."

"I'm a wealthy man. It may be someone after money. It may be more than that. I don't know." *I don't understand, either.* He was rich, and yet all his money hadn't been able to save Catherine five years ago. What if he lost someone he loved again? The feeling of having no control swamped him.

"A ransom? Someone wants to kidnap me?"

"That's a possibility."

"So that's why you freaked out at school."

"Yeah. Someone called with a threat against you. Then when no one could locate you…" His voice faded into the silence as he relived the fear he'd experienced when he couldn't find Abbey. The beating of his heart accelerated and sweat popped out on his forehead as though he were back in that school hallway at his daughter's classroom with no Abbey in it.

She glanced behind the car. "Why is that lady following us home?"

Another fortifying breath. "That lady is your bodyguard."

She bolted up. "What? A bodyguard?"

"Yes."

"She's gonna follow me around?"

"She will be with you at all times."

"When I go to school? The mall? To my friends'?"

"Yes." His throat dry, he swallowed hard and continued in a firm voice. "To school, but there won't be any mall trips. Your activities will be curtailed."

Abbey shook her head. "I'm grounded? I haven't done anything wrong."

At a stoplight he pinned her with a look that he hoped conveyed the seriousness of the situation. "This isn't about right and wrong. This is about your safety. You will do what Elizabeth Walker says. She'll be there to protect you."

"Protect me? I'm taller than she is. How's she gonna do that?"

"She works for Kyra, and Kyra highly recommends her. That's good enough for me." It had to be.

He was putting his daughter's life into Elizabeth's hands, and he hadn't trusted another person that way since Catherine.

"I'm not gonna have any privacy?"

"At home, to a certain degree. Whenever you're out, no."

"I don't have a say in this?"

"No," he bit out between gritted teeth, slanting a look at his daughter.

Her mouth was set in a stubborn line. She swung her full attention out the window and crossed her arms over her chest.

The rest of the fifteen-minute drive was done in silence. A silence Slade relished because any conversation he and Abbey had would end up in an argument.

When he arrived at the estate, he pushed his opener and waited for the gates to slowly swing open. As a boy, he'd wanted to be a cowboy, ride his horse and camp outside. That was why he'd bought the property. Yet this period of house arrest until the stalker was found would be the most waking hours he'd spent on the ranch in years.

Instead, he worked. If he worked hard enough, he didn't remember what he was missing or what he couldn't change—most of the time. But every once in a while he thought about his wife. Losing her had been devastating. How much more would he have to lose?

"Dad, the gate's open."

Blinking, he straightened and focused on the task at hand—drive the car to his house and meet with the sheriff. Try to make some kind of sense of all that was happening to him and his daughter. Try to figure out who was behind this. Because when he found the person responsible, that guy would regret ever coming after his family.

As he passed through the gates and navigated the road to his house, he peered at the red Trans Am behind his vehicle. He wasn't alone. He had help. Would it be enough?

Through the trees, the sight of his two-story white house with six columns across the front came into view—along with the sheriff's car and a black SUV. Standing on the large porch that ran the length of the front of the antebellum home were Hilda, Mary, the sheriff and an older gentleman who must be Joshua Walker. When Slade pulled up in the circular drive and parked behind the sheriff's vehicle, he slid his hands from the wheel and rubbed them on his pants. He couldn't deny the fear that blanketed him at the moment, but he wouldn't let others see it.

Abbey flounced out of the Lexus, and the slam of his passenger door prodded him to move. As he climbed from his car, Elizabeth parked her Trans Am behind his vehicle.

"You've got a nice little reception." She nodded

toward the porch as Abbey charged toward her grandmother, said something to her, then stomped to the black wicker settee a few yards away from the cluster of people in front of the open door. She plopped her book bag down by her feet.

"Yeah. You know, up until recently my life has been dull."

"I think that's about to change."

"Let's find out what happened here first. This might not be tied to the threats." He hoped this was the case, although he doubted it. "I'm afraid I waited too long to upgrade the security system."

Sheriff McCain ambled toward him and shook Slade's hand. "I just got here. I haven't had time to check the house out. I have a deputy checking the exterior, talking to your men. Hilda said she came home and found the front door wide open. Leaves had blown into the foyer. She walked inside and called out for Mary. When she didn't respond, Hilda got out of the house and placed a call to me."

"So you don't know if anything was taken?"

"She didn't see anything but didn't go very far in. Mary filled me in about the photo you found this morning at your office."

"I also received a threatening call against Abbey later at the office on my private line. I informed Captain Ted Dickerson of the Dallas police."

"I'll call him and let him know I have an interest in the case. We can coordinate our investigations."

"As you no doubt know," Slade said, gesturing toward Joshua then Elizabeth, "I've hired help. Ms. Walker will be Abbey's bodyguard while Mr. Walker will be guarding me. He's going to do a security assessment of my house today. Whatever it takes, I'll make this place a fortress."

"Good. You can never be too careful. I'm going inside and look around. You can come in when I think there isn't any danger."

"Okay." When he and the sheriff joined Hilda, Mary, Elizabeth and Joshua, Slade said to the group, "Sheriff McCain is going inside to make sure it's all right for us to go in." As the law enforcement officer moved toward the entrance, his hand on his holster, Slade glanced around. "Where's Jake?" Slade's foreman had been with him from the beginning, and he'd come to depend on him where the ranch was concerned. Jake would need to be kept informed because he knew this place better than most.

"I didn't get hold of him. No one answered at the barn, and I thought I shouldn't leave since the sheriff was on his way."

Slade nodded. "He said something about working on the fence in the north pasture. I'll let him know later what's going on if the deputy doesn't talk to him. I haven't had a chance to apprise him of the threats. As soon as we get the all clear, Joshua, I want you to start your assessment. It's obvious I could use more security." As his first security measure, he needed to make sure Jake had his cell on him at all times.

"Will do."

Slade peered at Abbey, who sat on the settee with her legs clasped to her chest, her chin resting on her knees. A pallor to her face, she looked shell-shocked. He made his way to his daughter and eased down beside her. "Okay?"

"Sure. What girl doesn't want a maniac after her and a twenty-four-hour bodyguard?"

He settled his hand on her shoulder. "I'm sorry, honey."

She shrugged away and turned toward him. Tears misted her eyes. "I've done nothing wrong, and yet I'm the one who's gonna feel like a prisoner. I just don't understand all this."

His heart twisted at the anguish in Abbey's voice, her expression. One tear slipped down her cheek. He brushed it away with the pad of his thumb. Abbey fell into his arms and hugged him.

He flashed back to the last few minutes before Catherine passed away. Tears had leaked from her closed eyes to course down her face—the same face as his daughter's. A stab of pain sliced through his defenses. His gaze linked with Elizabeth's, full of concern, and for a few seconds the hurt melted away.

The sheriff poked his head out the doorway. "All clear. It looks like everything is in its proper place, but Slade and Mary, you'll need to have a look around. At least for now, check the obvious things a thief would steal."

If the person after him and his daughter had been in his house, Slade felt exposed just sitting on the porch. He scanned the terrain, noting the horses grazing in the open field to the left, but a stand of trees directly in front would be a good place to hide. He'd prefer everyone inside. "Can we all come in?"

Sheriff McCain nodded and stood back from the entrance. "I need to check with my deputy and see if he found anything outside or if any of your men saw anyone."

Slade moved first into the house with Joshua on his heels. Abbey, Mary and Hilda followed with Elizabeth taking up the rear. Leaves littered the marble floor. A breeze from the door lifted several and swirled them around to land finally in the living room. He scanned the walls, making sure his couple of pieces of art were still hanging. The Manet over the mantel and the Degas between the two floor-to-ceiling windows were untouched. That fact relaxed the tense set of his shoulders and eased the roiling in his stomach. He'd bought the masterpieces for Catherine that last year she was so sick to cheer her up. She'd loved the impressionist period of art.

Maybe somehow the door wasn't latched properly

and the wind had blown it open. *Yeah, right, and maybe no one shot out your tire.*

As he tramped through his house with Joshua, checking the safe and other places he had valuables, he couldn't shake the sensation his life would never be the same. He'd learned in business to be wary. Now that feeling would overflow into his personal life.

Back in the foyer, Slade paused near the front door as the sheriff came back into the house. Any adrenaline that had surged through him had subsided, leaving him tired and in need of some caffeine. "I don't see anything missing," he said. "I'll check some more, but if nothing is missing, maybe no one was in here."

Joshua stepped next to him. "There are other reasons why someone would be in here. I'm going to do a sweep for bugs. I'll check your phones for any, too. I have my equipment out in the car."

Elizabeth joined them in the foyer while Mary and Abbey remained in the living room, sitting on the couch. "Your daughter wants to go up to her room."

"That's fine. Would you go with her and check it first? I looked in and didn't see anything, but a more thorough search would be better." Slade peered toward his daughter who sat with her shoulders hunched, her chin resting on her chest. "Then I'd like to meet with you and Joshua in my office."

* * *

Elizabeth stepped into Abbey's bathroom and surveyed the luxurious room done in beige marble with accents of forest green. Making the rounds, she opened and closed each cabinet and drawer, then headed back into the large bedroom. She checked for likely places someone would put a listening device, even though Joshua would do a more thorough scan of the whole house later.

Abbey stood in the middle with her arms folded over her chest and a glare on her face. "Don't forget under the bed."

"I won't." Elizabeth inspected the walk-in closet, twice as big as her bathroom at Joshua's.

"Oh, and I have a balcony."

Elizabeth left the closet, shutting the door. "That's a great suggestion," she said in the calmest voice she could muster. Teenage kids could be the most difficult to guard. They didn't like their privacy being invaded even for a good reason. She'd dealt with teens before, and she would deal with Abbey. The best way was to try to win her over, which might not be easy if her pout was any indication.

Before reaching the balcony, Elizabeth opened each drawer in her dresser, felt around, then shut it. The top one held a journal. Her fingers brushed over the bound book with horses on the front.

Abbey rushed toward her and snatched the journal out of the drawer. "That's private. Don't touch it." She glared at Elizabeth and hugged the book to her chest.

"I wouldn't look in it." She could remember the diary she'd kept as a teenager—many pages of angst. "Do you see anything missing or moved?"

Skimming her look over her possessions, Abbey backed away. She returned her razor-sharp attention to Elizabeth. "No."

Elizabeth swung open the French doors that led to the balcony and moved out into the December air, a stiff wind blowing the strands of her hair. Ten by ten with no easy access. Still, she would have Joshua wire the doors with sensors and secure them better.

True to her word, when she was back in the room she knelt on plush white carpet next to the king-size, dark-oak canopy bed with a hot-pink satin coverlet and looked under it. Nothing there but a single tennis shoe and one red sock.

When she rose, she peered at Abbey—the girl's posture was defensive, one hand quivering when she raised it to sweep her long brown hair behind her shoulders. The dark circles under the teen's eyes attested to the toll the past few days had taken on her. Something softened in Elizabeth. For a few seconds she recalled her own past fear, the feeling that the circumstances around her controlled her life. "All clear," she said to reassure Abbey.

"Oh, good, I'm relieved to know there are no

monsters under it. I quit looking for them when I was eight."

"I know this can't be easy, but I'm here to help you."

"Don't pretend you know what this feels like. I'm a prisoner."

Elizabeth panned the room that lacked nothing, from a big-screen TV to a state-of-the art computer and sound system. "Not too bad a cell."

Abbey snorted. "Are you satisfied everything is okay? I'd like to be alone, if that's all right. Surely I can be alone in my own cell—I mean, bedroom."

"I'll be downstairs in your dad's office."

"Oh, good. That's right below me. I'll stomp on the floor if I need you."

As Elizabeth made her way down to Slade's office, she clung to the image of Abbey out on the porch. A young girl on the verge of falling apart and trying desperately not to—even using anger to keep herself together. Elizabeth did know what that felt like. But at least Abbey's father had been right there for her. The love and worry in his expression reached out to Elizabeth and gripped her heart. How many times had she prayed to see something like that on her own father's face?

She rapped on the office door. When she heard Slade say, "Enter," she went inside. He sat in a chair behind his desk, swiveled around to face a large window that framed two horses frolicking in the pasture.

"Right now I can't remember a time when I spent a day just playing, with not a worry in the world."

The weariness in his voice beckoned her forward. "It's been a while for me, too." Even as a child she'd never felt totally free to be herself, to enjoy life without a concern. The thought made loneliness creep into her heart.

He rotated his chair around. His gaze snagged hers, intensity in his gray eyes and something else—vulnerability—that reached out to her, linking them. Her pulse reacted by speeding through her.

"I guess that's a price we pay when we grow up." He cocked a corner of his mouth in a half grin that faded almost instantly. "But my daughter shouldn't have to worry about it quite yet."

The appeal in those startling eyes, storm-filled at the moment, touched a place in her heart that she'd kept firmly closed for years. She wrenched her look away and swept around in a full circle. "Nice office." Which was putting it mildly. From a huge mahogany desk with a large-screen computer to the sumptuous brown leather grouping along one side of the room to the floor-to-ceiling bookcases on the other wall, the office was luxurious to the extreme.

He rose. "Let's have a seat over there where it's

comfortable. Joshua's doing a walk-through with Mary. How was Abbey?"

"Not a happy camper."

"I figured that. When she gets scared, she gets angry. The first year after her mother died, I thought my home was a war zone. Thankfully, she began to accept her mother's death, and I nearly had my daughter back. Then she hit puberty. Everything changed. Did I tell you I don't like change?"

"I'll tell you a secret. Neither do I."

"How do you do what you do?"

"One assignment at a time. It's important for me to keep my focus on the present." And she had to remember that. No more journeys into her past.

He took one end of the couch and beckoned her to sit at the other end. "I'm glad it's Tuesday. I have the Thanksgiving holidays before Abbey goes back to school to get things worked out. It'll give you two some time to get to know each other. To get her used to you being around."

"We'll get into a routine. That should help."

At that moment Uncle Joshua entered with Slade's mother-in-law, a woman in her early sixties with short silver hair and dark brown eyes. She came to right above Joshua's shoulders, and he was well over six feet tall.

Dressed in stylish tan slacks and a matching jacket and a white tailored blouse, Mary grasped the back of one of the chairs in the grouping while

Joshua folded his long length into the opposite one. "Hilda is still shaken up in the kitchen," she said. "I'll be in there if you need me."

"I appreciate the tour, Mary." Joshua grinned, his look fastened onto the older woman.

Mary's cheeks colored a pink shade as she scurried from the room.

Joshua chuckled. "I don't think she's too comfortable with everything."

"She hasn't had much time to assimilate what's going on. I only called her a few hours ago to tell her my plans. Until then, all she thought was that we'd had a blowout on Saturday. She's lived a pretty sheltered life, especially here at the ranch." Slade shifted on the couch as though he couldn't get settled. "I thought we should talk about some kind of game plan."

Joshua tapped his fingers on the arm of the chair, something he did when he was impatient to get to work. "As I told you before, I want to check for listening devices, then talk to the people who put in your security system."

"I want to get a feel for the house and the surrounding area. Meet the people who work for you besides Hilda." Elizabeth captured Slade's attention. "Everyone."

"That's fine. I can introduce—"

A scream from above ripped through the house, followed by a thud.

FOUR

The scream coming from his daughter slammed Slade's heart against his chest. He bolted to his feet and rushed for the door. Elizabeth wrenched it open a few strides in front of him.

The silence that followed Abbey's shriek quickened his pace. Bounding up the stairs, Elizabeth pulled her gun from her holster. Several steps back, Joshua withdrew his, too. The sight of the weapons sent ice through Slade's veins.

At the top of the staircase, Slade surged around Elizabeth, determined to get to Abbey. Thoughts of what could be happening raced through his mind, threatening to paralyze him. He silenced them and kept going down the long hallway to Abbey's room at the end—the longest fifteen yards he'd ever covered.

Nearing his daughter's bedroom, Elizabeth clamped her hand on his elbow. "Let me go in first."

Common sense told him to agree, but the father

in him couldn't. Shaking off her grasp, he increased his speed and shoved open the door, charging inside. He came to a halt a few feet in. Abbey stood in front of her computer, the chair toppled over behind her. Her face bleached of color, she twisted toward him. Her mouth opened but no sound came from it.

Ignoring Joshua and Elizabeth behind him, he crossed the room and clasped his daughter's arms. "What's wrong?"

Tears flooded her wide eyes. "My computer." She launched herself at him and clung to him, her whole body trembling.

Slade swung his gaze to the computer. The sight on it curdled his gut. The screen was totally black except for Abbey's name written across it in a font that looked like blood that dripped and pooled at the bottom. The horror of what he saw and its implication took over, erasing all thoughts.

Abbey's sobs against his chest finally brought him out of his daze. He tried to move her away, but she remained rooted to the floor, clutching him as though he were her life preserver. "Honey, what happened?" he whispered against her hair.

For a long moment she continued to cry. Then, slowly she quieted, gulping in shallow breaths that finally deepened. Her body still quaking, she drew back, her eyes glistening with her tears. "I turned on my computer, and that is what popped up on the screen. How? Why?"

He glanced again at the computer, chilled at what he saw. When Abbey started to look at it, he blocked her view. "I don't know, but I intend to find out."

"Slade? Abbey? What's going on?" Mary stood in the entrance to his daughter's bedroom, her forehead creased with worry.

"We'll look into this," Elizabeth said, stepping forward. "Why don't you take Abbey out of here?"

Slade peered at her, hearing the words but not registering them for a few seconds. She'd holstered her gun, as had Joshua, but that didn't lessen the implication that someone had possibly been in Abbey's room and that the maniac, as Abbey called him, was involved in what happened earlier. Elizabeth was right. Abbey needed to leave.

"Come on, Abbey. Let's go downstairs and let Elizabeth and Joshua check this out."

"Daddy?"

Her tears welled up and ran down her cheeks. Seeing them and feeling so helpless broke Slade's heart. He wound his arm around her shoulder and walked her toward Mary. His mother-in-law's expression grew more concerned when she caught sight of Abbey's face, her shaking body.

As he left with them, Slade threw a glance at Elizabeth. "I want answers." Because no matter what, he would find the maniac and make him pay for what he was doing to Abbey.

* * *

"I want answers, too," Elizabeth said to Joshua after the trio left them alone in Abbey's bedroom. "Was this the point of the break-in earlier? To put something on her computer?"

"A scare tactic? Could be."

"It worked. Abbey was scared." And the expression in Slade's eyes spoke of his fear but also his fury, barely contained. The urge to comfort him stunned Elizabeth. She didn't get emotionally involved in her assignments, and yet she couldn't get his earlier expression of fear and fury out of her mind.

"I have a tech consultant I use. I'll call him out here to see if it was loaded in from here or if somehow the person hacked into Abbey's computer." Joshua dug into his pocket for his cell.

"So let's leave this alone and get him out here."

"Then I need to secure this place. Slade's security system isn't state-of-the art. I've found a lot of things that need beefing up, and I'm not even done with the assessment." He punched a number into the phone, but hadn't yet placed the call when Slade returned.

"I can find out how it got on Abbey's computer. I'm pretty sure it had to be placed there physically, because my firewall on the computer system we use here is top-notch, but I know how to find out for sure."

"Okay, then I'll leave you here to check it out. I have work to do on the rest of the house." Joshua left the bedroom.

"Where's Abbey?"

"She's lying down in Mary's suite. I explained to Mary what happened and that I would be in here." Slade righted the chair and sat in front of the computer.

As his fingers flew over the keys, the black screen with Abbey's name disappeared to be replaced with an entry box. Listening to him mumble to himself, as though he were coaxing the computer to give him the right answers, Elizabeth couldn't help admiring his skills—ones she lacked.

After a minute of watching him go from one area to another, she began to walk around the room, trying to imagine the intruder in the room. Although she'd checked the area out earlier, she did again, praying she hadn't missed anything obvious. If the person had come in here to put that on the computer, why had he risked doing it? What was his objective? Was there anything else he did in the house? One question after another tumbled through her mind, each leaving her with a bad feeling about the situation.

So far, it wasn't motivated by the need for money. Malice seemed to lay behind the person's actions. A score to settle? Very possibly.

Stepping out on the balcony again, Elizabeth

swept her gaze over the landscape. In the distance she glimpsed a black barn. A woman with curly blonde hair exited it. A man wearing a black cowboy hat, boots and jeans led a horse from the barn. The woman whirled around and kissed the wrangler on the mouth before she headed away in the opposite direction. Seeing the two reinforced Elizabeth's need to meet each person who worked at the ranch. She didn't know who belonged and who didn't.

Going back inside, she left Slade inputting on the computer while she went to Mary's suite to check on Abbey. Mary's living quarters were next to her room. She knocked on its door and waited.

When Slade's mother-in-law let her into the sitting room, Elizabeth surveyed the beautifully decorated area, noting the entrance to the bedroom off to the left. "Is Abbey in there?"

Mary nodded.

Elizabeth strode to the open doorway and peeked in. The teenager lay on a huge king size sleigh bed, curled up in a ball, her eyes closed.

"She's exhausted," Mary whispered behind Elizabeth and pulled the door closed before facing her. "I'm so worried about her. First the wreck and now this. What could make a person so vile that he'd want to harm my family? I feel helpless. I'm so glad Slade hired you to watch out for Abbey. If Kyra recommends you, then that's all I need to know.

You'll do your best. My daughter and Kyra were best friends in high school. Inseparable."

Elizabeth journeyed back to her days in high school and couldn't remember having a friend like that. Her father didn't like her bringing friends home, and he didn't allow her to participate in many activities because her studies were too important. She had to be at the top of her class, and if she wasn't, he let her know how disappointed he was in her. A mental shake rid her mind of those memories. She couldn't afford to get sidetracked on this job.

"I'll do my best, Mrs. Bradley."

"Mary. We've never stood on formality at this ranch."

She recalled the cowboy and the blonde earlier. "I haven't had a chance to ask Slade yet, but who besides Hilda works in the house?"

"Hilda's daughter comes in three times a week to help her mother clean."

"Does Hilda live here?"

"Yes, and she's been a dear friend since I came here." Mary frowned. "She doesn't have anything to do with this. You're wasting your time going down that trail."

"I have to consider everything, even what seems unlikely, if for no other reason than to rule it out." She didn't tell Mary that she hadn't ruled out Hilda yet. It was safer to suspect everyone.

"I know, dear, but she's been with the family since Abbey was born."

"Who left first today, you or Hilda?"

"She did. This is her day to go into town and run all her errands. Most times she is gone for hours."

"Does she do it every Tuesday?"

Mary tilted her head. "Why, yes, she does."

"Do you usually go to church on Tuesday?"

"No, I usually work at home putting together the church bulletin. I hole myself up in Slade's office, but the secretary needed help at church today so I put it off. Her husband fell and needed to go to the doctor."

"So Hilda expected you to be here?"

Mary nodded.

"When you left, you turned the alarm on?"

Her eyebrows crunched together as Mary peered over Elizabeth's shoulder. "I'm sure I did. I know I was in a hurry to get to church, but I don't think I forgot." Her gaze returned to Elizabeth's face. "Do you think I left the house open?"

"I don't know, but the door was open and the alarm didn't go off."

Mary's eyes widened. She brought her hand up to cover her mouth. "Oh, no."

Elizabeth hated seeing the woman's look of regret and patted her arm. "That's only one possible explanation."

"What else could explain it?"

"Someone knows the alarm code and has a key to the house. Or someone was already in the house when you left and turned the alarm off."

"They would have to know the code."

"True. How many people know it?"

"I'm not sure."

"Have you changed it lately?"

"No, I haven't." Slade's deep voice sounded from the doorway.

Elizabeth spun around to face him, her heart reacting to his commanding presence. "When was the last time you did?"

"Not since I moved in."

"Then I would change it right away and not give it out."

"Certain people need to have it."

"Who?"

"Hilda, Abbey, Mary and Jake."

"Isn't Jake your foreman? Why him?"

"My office here is also the office for the ranch. He comes up here to work several days a week. I suppose we'll have to make different arrangements since I'll be working from home for the time being." He looked toward Mary. "Is Abbey still lying down?"

His mother-in-law eased the door into the bedroom open, then closed it quietly. "Yes."

"Good. Elizabeth and I need to talk. Can you

keep an eye on Abbey? I don't want her to wake up alone."

"She won't." Mary bent over and grabbed a knitting bag, then ambled into the other room.

"What did you find on the computer?" Elizabeth asked as they left Mary's suite.

"Someone physically put it on the computer, which means he was in the house." He strode to the staircase and descended. "We need to finish our strategy meeting from earlier. Can you find your uncle and meet me in my office while I go change the alarm code?"

"Yes." Elizabeth parted from him in the foyer in search of Uncle Joshua.

She found him in the kitchen talking with Hilda. "Slade wants to meet with us in his office."

"Okay," he said before turning his focus back to Hilda. "Jones Cartwright and his men will be here soon to replace the doors and locks. I'd appreciate it if you would let them in and then let me know."

Hilda nodded. "I can do that. Anything else I can do just tell me."

When they left the kitchen, Elizabeth chuckled. "What have you been telling her? Stories of your days on the police force?"

Joshua grunted. "I don't have time for that, but it's important to get the cooperation of the members of the staff and family. We don't know what's going on here."

"Slade discovered someone was in Abbey's bedroom. That's how that image got on her computer."

"I was hoping that wasn't the case."

"Yeah, we've got to shut down this person's access to the house."

"And check the people who work for Slade."

"And have been here in the past month or two, especially anyone new."

"Which means all his employees here at the ranch." Joshua pushed open the door to Slade's office, and Elizabeth entered first to find Slade staring out the large window behind his desk.

"I'm thinking of moving my desk away from the window." Slade rotated toward them.

"Wouldn't hurt." Joshua took the chair he'd occupied an hour ago. "I'd keep exposure limited, if possible. We can look at using bullet-resistant glass where necessary if you want."

"I'm already beginning to feel like my daughter. That we're living in a prison." Slade skirted his desk and took a seat on the couch, leaning back. But there was nothing casual or at ease about his posture. Rigidity locked his muscles in place. Even his hands were fisted. "I need this place secure as soon as possible, so whatever you think is best, do it."

"The good thing is, we can do a lot to enhance your present system, such as a control panel that handles your downstairs needs and one for your upstairs." Joshua looked down at the pad he held. "Add laser beams, put more sensors around to cover every door and window, new locks and sturdier doors. I'm taking care of that today. For the alarm system, change your code weekly. Don't give it out to anyone but the people who live in the house or need to know. Keep that list short."

Slade winced. "It's obvious my security wasn't that good. It's never been an issue. This is the first time I've ever had any trouble."

Still standing, Elizabeth clasped the back of the chair in front of her. "Have you thought about sending Abbey away? Mary, too?"

Slade bent forward, his elbows on his thighs, his hands gripped together. "What would stop the stalker from going after Abbey wherever she went? He could find out where I sent her."

"I'd be with her."

"No. At least here, we can control things more. If someone wants to do the most harm to me, coming after my daughter is the way. And I think this person knows that." Slade turned to Joshua. "I want you to bring in some non-uniformed security personnel to patrol the grounds so this place won't feel so much like a prison." He waved his hand toward the large picture window. "I don't want my family being afraid to walk in front of a window. And living in a dark, closed-up house isn't the answer either, so whatever you think is necessary to let us move around the house freely is fine with me. Whatever it takes to have as normal a life as possible. I'm leaving it in your hands."

"I'll do what is needed," Joshua said, jotting something down on the pad. "I'd also suggest adding a panic room in case someone does breach the security."

"Okay." He flexed his balled hands slowly. "I read once that having a dog was a good deterrent. What do you think?"

"It wouldn't hurt. I have a friend who used to be on the force who trains guard dogs. Do you want me to have him bring over a couple for you to look at?" Joshua stood.

"Yes."

"I've got some calls to make to get this in motion. You'll have new doors and locks today. The rest can be in place by the end of the weekend, except the panic room. That might take longer since it's Thanksgiving in two days."

As her uncle headed toward the door, Elizabeth took a seat in the chair. Slade's haggard look matched the expressions of a lot parents she had dealt with, and they always touched her. But in this case something else wheedled its way into her heart, knocking down her defenses.

Slade dropped his head into his palms and scrubbed them down his face. When his gaze reconnected with hers, a stark bleakness peered back at her. For a long moment it robbed her of her voice. The yearning to sit next to him and clasp his hands almost overwhelmed her.

"Tell me about Abbey. Help me to understand her. The faster I can get to know her, the better job I can do protecting her," Elizabeth finally said to take his mind off his thoughts.

"What do you think so far?"

"I don't think she likes the idea of having a bodyguard. Of having someone invade her privacy."

"I figured that. She used to share everything with me. Now I can hardly find out how her day has gone. I know that can be pretty typical of a teenager, but I want my daughter back, the one who came to me with every little problem and asked my opinion. The one who…" His voice melted into a raw huskiness.

If only her father had felt that kind of love for her, what would her childhood have been like? Would they still be strangers today? Emotions swelled into her throat, and she cleared it in order to continue. "She likes drama, basketball and cheerleading. Anything else?"

"Animals, especially horses. For a while she was showing horses but got away from that when she hit high school and became more involved with the other activities. But she does like to ride, especially on the weekend when she has more time."

"Maybe she would like a little dog. The kind that makes a lot of noise when people come around. The guard dogs could be for the grounds, but the little one for inside the house."

He rolled his shoulders and eased against the back cushion. "I'll see what she says. Her dog of thirteen years died last year, and she hasn't been ready for a new one. She might like one now."

"Or better yet, I have a terrier mix named Bosco. I could bring him here. The boy next door to my uncle watches him when we can't. Bosco is well trained but also barks at anything out of the ordinary. One of the best little watchdogs. It might be hard finding one that will do what we need. I know Bosco will."

"Great, that would be better. Then if Abbey enjoys having Bosco around, I'll get her a dog of her own when all this is over with."

"Anything else about Abbey I should know?"

"She's creative and especially kind to underdogs, but she's also a drama queen and impulsive. She does things without thinking, and as I said before, she takes unnecessary risks. She's got a lot of friends—girls and boys."

"She isn't dating?"

"Not as far as I know. When she goes out, a bunch of them go out together in a large group. Male and female."

"I suggest we don't do any of that for the time being."

"That won't sit well with her."

"Even after what happened today with her computer?"

Slade sighed. "A week from now she'll have forgotten her terror at seeing that. If nothing happens between now and then, she'll think it's safe for her to go out with her friends."

"School is manageable," Elizabeth said. "They have a security system in place, and with me there she should be okay, especially if we use one of the security guards to drive us to and from Dawson Academy. That'll allow me to keep my attention totally focused on the surroundings, not divide it between that and driving. It won't be as much fun as going out with friends, but at least it'll get her out of the house. This will work out."

The tension in his body dissolved some. He stretched his arm along the back of the couch and pinned her with an inquiring look. "You're good at your job. What made you become a bodyguard?"

"Because I like challenges."

"The challenge of protecting people?"

"That, too, but what drew me to the profession was all the training I would have to complete to be good at my job." Training that would ensure no one took advantage of her again. She let her gaze travel down her short frame. "As you pointed out this morning, I'm not what someone would think of when you mention a bodyguard. I had a few obstacles to overcome. That was the challenge I wanted. My previous life was nothing like this one."

"What was it like?"

She'd been a doormat, but she wasn't going to say that to this man. She hadn't shared her past with anyone except Uncle Joshua. "The most dangerous thing I did was climb up on a ladder to change a lightbulb."

He chuckled. "No safety net?"

"None. Wasn't that daring?" She smiled, relaxing her own tension.

"Very. So you went from changing lightbulbs to carrying a gun and using tae kwon do on anyone who dared to cross you. Interesting. But something tells me there's a story in there you aren't telling me." His gaze pierced through the armor she hid herself in. "And the very fact that you aren't telling me intrigues me."

The heat from his look blazed through her as though he'd cut through her shield with a laser. She immediately redirected the conversation. "I know the police are going to be investigating your case, but I'd like to try and figure out who has a grudge against you. Any ideas on that?"

"You don't like talking about yourself."

It wasn't a question, but Elizabeth said, "Boring subject."

"Ah, I doubt that. I did a little checking on your score on the weapon test. I realize how good that is, not to mention the third degree black belt. I saw you in action at the school. You were constantly scanning your surroundings, always aware, alert. Most people don't do that. It seems to come naturally to you. I have a feeling if I asked you to close your eyes and describe this office, you could to a tee."

Elizabeth shut her eyes. "To my right is your mahogany desk, three feet by six, with a Mac computer sitting to the left of the middle. On the other side is a beige mobile phone, a calendar, a frame with a photograph of Abbey that I would say was taken recently. A stack of folders sits square in the middle of your tan-colored blotter with a black and silver pen next to it. Your chair is medium brown leather that looks soft and expensive. Behind the desk to the right there is a high-end printer, fax, scanner—wireless, apparently, since there's no cable going from your computer to it. Then on—"

"You've convinced me." His laughter infused the words. "Actually, you really didn't have to."

When she opened her eyes, he'd risen and hovered over her, all six feet plus of his powerful body. His close proximity sent her pulse hammering. For several rapid heartbeats, she remained still, drawing in his distinctive male scent of soap and something all his own. Tantalizing. Captivating.

He held out his hand to her. She stared at it for

a few more rapid heartbeats, then stood, sidling away to the right. When she was finally a couple of feet from him, her bodily reactions to his nearness calmed. What was happening here? He was her employer. Nothing more than that.

"I need to see if Abbey has awakened yet. It's time we got to know each other since we'll be spending a lot of time together." The rasp to her voice announced the effect he was having on her. She gritted her teeth, determined to keep her distance.

She turned away to go to the door. A hand clamped about her arm, stopping her progress forward. She glanced at the long, strong fingers that clasped her. When she raised her gaze to his, she arched a brow.

"Thanks for taking the job. I've got a feeling I may need all the help I can get before this is over with."

The worry that weaved through his words stilled her automatic reaction to go on the offense, to yank her arm from his grasp. She gave him a grin and said, "You're welcome."

The office door slammed open with such force it bounced against the wall.

FIVE

Abbey charged into the room, her eyes spitting fire, her mouth compressed into a frown. "Dad, I have a basketball game tonight. I can't miss that. Gram told me I couldn't go."

Beside him, Elizabeth—who had instantly become alert, her hand going to her weapon at her waist—relaxed, moving away from his touch. The severed contact left him feeling cold.

"Dad, I'm a cheerleader. I have to go."

"I think it's best with all that has happened for you to stay home tonight. We're still trying to figure out how to keep everyone safe. I can't let anything happen to you, honey."

"I'm letting the squad down. I can't."

"They'll understand. You were in a wreck a few days ago. If you want I'll call your sponsor and explain."

Abbey's eyes grew round. "No! I'll do it." She looked from him to Elizabeth. "Is it safe for me to go back into my room?"

"I'll go with you." Elizabeth stepped forward.

"No, I've got to have some privacy." Abbey swept her attention back to Slade. "Did you take that—that thing off my computer?"

He shook his head. "I want the sheriff to look at it. He's coming by in a little while to take it with him. You can use my laptop in my room for the time being."

"Fine." His daughter huffed then swung around and stomped out of the office.

"I'd better follow."

"Did I forget to tell you she is headstrong?"

"I kind of figured that one out for myself." Elizabeth left.

The image of her smile, which reached deep into her eyes and caused them to gleam, stayed with him as he trudged toward his desk. A stack of personnel folders, all of people who had been fired in the past year, sat on top of his blotter in front of him. While he waited for the sheriff to show up, he'd go through each file and see who he might have angered enough to want to hurt him and his family.

Late that night, Elizabeth came down the stairs and went to the security panel near the new steel-reinforced front door. After checking to make sure the alarm system was still on, she made her way through the first floor to find Uncle Joshua. He stood at the bay window in the kitchen nook, staring outside into the darkness.

"Tomorrow I'm having more motion sensitive lights installed outside. By the time I'm through, it will be hard to approach the house at night without setting one off. Right now there are some spots that still remain dark." Joshua turned toward her.

"So that was what you were doing outside tonight. Figuring out where those spots were." The dark shadows under his eyes concerned her. "You need to go to bed. It's been a long day, and it's two-thirty in the morning."

"I'll feel better when I've completed updating the security system tomorrow."

"You can't stay up all night and function tomorrow. There are two guards outside patrolling with their dogs."

"I know, but this is a big place."

"Get some sleep. You don't have to worry. I'll stay up now."

"But what about you?" He pulled the blinds shut and moved away from the window.

"I got over four hours of sleep. I feel fine. You know how I am in a new place. It takes me a while to get used to it. I never sleep as well as I usually do."

"Still…"

"Uncle Joshua, all the outside doors have been changed to high tempered steel ones and the jambs reinforced. All the locks are three-inch deadbolts. The security code was changed. You found three listening devices and sent them to the sheriff to see if he can track down where they came from. For only being on the job half a day, you've accomplished a lot." She took his arm and led him toward the hallway. "Go to bed. There will be a lot going on in five hours."

"If you need me, my cell will be on the bedside table."

She smiled, hooking her arm through his. "And I've got you on speed dial." At the staircase she paused. "This will give me a good chance to get even better acquainted with this house while Abbey is asleep."

Joshua looked around at the foyer, which was open to the second floor, with a large crystal chandelier hanging down from the two story ceiling. "And this is a huge house."

"Seven bedrooms, nine bathrooms, a media room, formal living room, dining room, kitchen, den, library and a large office. Not to mention a to-die-for exercise room and indoor lap pool."

"Nothing you haven't seen before. So many of the clients you've worked for have a lot of money."

"But not too many have been down-to-earth. Not like…" She couldn't voice the confusing feelings she had for her employer. He was very wealthy, but when the workmen came today to change the doors and locks, he was right there helping them. Then later he'd greeted his foreman as though they were good friends, not employer/employee. Hilda was treated like a member of his family. After her last difficult assignment, where her employer barely spoke to her, Slade's attitude was refreshing.

Joshua studied her for a long moment. "You like him, don't you?"

"Yes. I sense a vulnerability in him. Things haven't been easy for him."

"An easy life isn't all it's cracked up to be. Think how soft we would be."

"Probably wouldn't make me a very good body-guard."

"Good night." Joshua squeezed her hand, then ascended the stairs to the second floor.

Elizabeth watched her uncle disappear down the hallway, then slowly rotated toward the large, round, cherry table in the center of the room-size foyer. Fresh flowers—lilies, roses and some she didn't know the name of—perfumed the air with a light sweetness that reminded her of spring.

Where would she be when spring came? In another state? Another country? Chances were, not in Dallas. She heaved a sigh. That was what she wanted. To travel. To not depend on anyone but herself. To test herself constantly, honing her skills.

Then why did she feel empty, as though something was missing from her life?

She was doing everything she'd promised herself when she put the pieces of her shattered life back together after Bryan left, after her father's final rejection. No regrets.

With a sigh, she started her trek through the first floor, noting every window and door, especially the ones that led outside. By the time she arrived at Slade's office, an hour had passed, and still restless energy surged through her. She walked to the door that opened on the east side of the house and tested it to make sure it was locked. Noticing that Slade had moved his desk away from the one large window in the room, she went to his chair and checked its placement. Another foot toward the wall would be better. She positioned herself in front to shove the desk. It scraped across the wooden floor.

"Do you need any help?"

The sound of Slade's deep, gravelly voice swung her around to face him in the entrance, where he was lounging against the doorjamb, his arms loosely folded over his T-shirt-clad chest, a light in his eyes. "No, I've got it."

"Didn't like where I put it?"

She straightened, leaning back against the desk, her hands clasping its edge. The sight of him weakened her knees. Dressed in sweats, his hair tousled, he looked comfortable, nothing like the successful businessman she'd met that morning. "You can still see outside, but the angle is better. It would be harder for someone to see you."

"Why thank you, ma'am, for thinking of me."

His Texan drawl curled her toes. She immediately erected her defenses. She'd been married before to a man who at first had been charming. Everything had changed after they were wedded. She'd become a possession to him—one that, in the end, he'd easily discarded. Her fingers dug into the wood of the desk.

Slade shoved away from the door frame and slowly covered the space between them. His gaze linked with hers and that was all she saw. Her heartbeat kicked up a notch at the predatory gleam in his eyes. She wanted to speak to defuse the tension, but her parched throat from Slade's intense look stole any reply.

She felt vulnerable, and it had nothing to do with someone wanting to hurt her. There was something about Slade that appealed to her. His physical presence was compelling, but what really moved her was his care for the people he loved. When she witnessed him with Abbey today, the love and acceptance she'd seen in his eyes reinforced what she'd missed in her own childhood. When he talked about his daughter, she heard it in his voice, even when he was upset with Abbey. The love was there no matter what. Her uncle was the only one who had shown her that kind of love, and before today, she'd thought that was enough.

He stopped just short of her personal space. "I never thought of how vulnerable I could be until Joshua went over his list of changes this evening. And when he found that bug in here, and two more downstairs, it nailed home that this whole situation isn't going away anytime soon."

"We might find out something from the sheriff about where the listening devices were purchased. That could be just the break we need. We want you and Abbey to feel safe when you're at home. Today was a beginning. This situation will be hard enough even with this place becoming a stronghold." With her hands aching from her tight grip, she loosened her clasp on the edge of the desk and took a steadying breath.

"Yeah, I know. Abbey wasn't too happy about not being able to go to the game tonight. She asked me earlier when I went to talk to her in her bedroom why had I hired you if she couldn't leave the ranch. I promised her she could go to school, at least, with you right there to keep her safe. That way she can see her friends. I'm not sure she has really grasped that someone is after her, even with what she saw on her computer."

"Will you allow her friends to come here?"

"Yes, the ones I know. She already asked if she could have the cheerleading squad here to practice.

I think she feels this will all be over in a week or so, and her life will go back to normal."

"I hope it will."

The intensity in his look increased. "But you don't think so."

"It depends on how fast the police can find this person. Otherwise the threat is still out there, even if nothing happens for a while. I've seen people lured into a sense of safety, then their world falls totally apart."

"That's why I brought home the personnel files of the people who were fired at DDI in the past year." He pointed toward the folders on his desk, the action bringing him a few inches closer to Elizabeth. "I'm not going to sit by idly and wait for the police to find this person. I'm going to do what I can to figure it out. Christmas is in five weeks, and I hope this can be solved by then. Christmas is a big deal for Mary and Abbey."

"Do you want some help going through your files?" she asked before she realized she would be committing herself to working with Slade when she wasn't with Abbey.

The corners of his mouth slowly lifted. "I was hoping you and Joshua would. I'm not a detective, but I can't sit by and do nothing."

"I'm not either, but I've picked up a few things while working as a bodyguard and just being around Joshua. Have you gone through the files yet?" She took a side step so she could partially face the desk as though she were only intent on the folders. But that wasn't the case. She was aware of every movement Slade made—when he kneaded his neck muscles or ran his finger across his wedding band.

"Yes, but nothing really jumps out at me."

"How many were fired in the past year?"

"Only seven in Texas, but twenty-nine worldwide. I was concentrating on the ones in Texas."

"Don't. Anger makes people do many things— even hop on a plane and come to Dallas if their intended target is here."

He blew a breath out. "That's why I won't let Abbey and Mary leave here. I need them close to make sure they're as safe as they can be. I'll have my secretary deliver the other files on Monday, but I thought I should start with these."

"What about people you fired before this year?"

He crunched his shoulders up, rubbing his hand along his nape. "The list could get long if we went back years."

"A lot of them can probably be eliminated pretty fast. I think starting with the most recent ones is good, but we can't rule out anyone."

"What if it isn't someone I fired?"

"That needs to be considered, too."

His tense shoulders sagged as though the enormity

of the task had suddenly overwhelmed him. The urge to comfort him swept through Elizabeth, and it took all her willpower not to touch his arm.

"So what do you think we should do first?" he asked, straightening to his full height.

"Take the people fired this year and find out what they're doing, where they are at this moment. If nothing turns up, we can broaden our scope."

"Then you should take a look at these seven. Maybe an objective perspective would help to flag anything suspicious." He leaned forward to retrieve the files from his desktop.

His sleeve grazed her. An electric jolt streaked up her arm as if she'd been shocked. Then, when he presented the folders to her, their hands brushed and the sensation of being burned caused her to yank the files back against her chest. She lifted her gaze at the same time he did and became ensnared by his. He'd felt the same physical reaction as she had. It was clear in the depth of his eyes, a slight widening, a few lines appearing on his forehead. He stepped back, twirling his wedding band while she clutched the files against her.

"While I'm up," she said, licking her dry lips, "this will help pass the time."

"You couldn't sleep either?"

"Joshua and I decided to split the night. Have one of us awake downstairs just in case anything happened."

"Why? There are guards patrolling the grounds."

"We'll feel better when the house is more secure." She backed up a few paces, needing more space between them. She could see why he'd become so successful in his business. Like Joshua, he commanded respect. But someone out there didn't care.

"I couldn't sleep. I kept seeing Abbey's name on her computer. Someone had changed her background so they would terrify her when she booted it up. That was personal. Not a competitor."

"Yes, and because they have involved you, the person they intended to hurt is most likely you."

"I agree, but I suppose we can't totally rule out someone just after Abbey."

"Is there anyone you can think of who might be angry at both of you?"

"I don't think…" He frowned. His eyes took on a faraway look, as if he was remembering something from the past. "I can't believe I didn't think about this. There was a boy who had a crush on Abbey last winter. When I discovered him trespassing on my property, I called the sheriff. He and his dad weren't too happy about that, but he stopped bothering Abbey. She told me he wasn't at Dawson Academy anymore. I thought they had moved away from Dallas."

"Who is it? He needs to be checked out. This has a feel of a stalker."

"Kevin Sharpe. I'll let the sheriff know."

"Is there anyone else you can think of?"

He shook his head. "At least I don't think so." He funneled his fingers through his hair. "But right now I'm questioning everything."

"I know how hard this can be." She moved closer, drawn by the frustration and pain on his face. "Try not to force it. I find myself shutting down when I do. I'll talk with Abbey about this Kevin guy and see if she's thought of anyone else since we talked last."

Weariness dulled his eyes like unpolished silver. "What else am I forgetting? I feel like I know something important and can't remember it."

The anguish in his voice compelled her to cut the distance between them and place her fingers on his arm. She held the files out. "This is a great start. Whatever we find, we can let the sheriff and Captain Dickerson know. You've got a lot of people who want to find this person."

He covered her hand. The deep look he gave her eroded her composure. For a moment time ceased, her attention traveling down to his lips, slightly parted. Sucking in a sharp breath, Elizabeth severed their tactile connection and backed away.

"I still have the den to check." Without waiting for him to say anything, she hurried toward the doorway.

"I'll make a pot of coffee. Let's review the files together."

Like a team popped into her mind and heightened her concern that she had just crossed into territory that was more dangerous than having a killer after her.

Four hours and many cups of coffee later, Elizabeth sat at the kitchen table with the folders spread out as she and Slade made a list of people to check out. Kevin Sharpe topped that list with three of the ex-employees as definite seconds.

Slade collapsed back against the chair. "I think we accomplished something here."

"It gives the police a place to start."

"Not us?"

She pushed to her feet and walked to the coffeepot on the counter. "More?"

He shook his head. "I'm wired as it is."

After pouring her mug full of the strong brew, Elizabeth came back and took her seat next to Slade at the round glass table. "It won't hurt for us to look into these people, too." It was important for people being threatened to feel they were doing something about their circumstances. And she didn't have a problem with that as long as they weren't put in harm's way. "The internet is a good place to start."

"You sound like you've done this before."

"A few times. The more information you have, the less likely you'll be surprised." She never wanted to be put in that situation again. Bryan's affair shouldn't have astounded her, but she'd been naive, hoping for the best. She didn't do that anymore.

"Who's taken you by surprise?"

Bryan's name was on the tip of her tongue, but she clamped down her teeth and kept it to herself. She didn't expose her past to others. "You don't need to worry. No one in my job as a bodyguard." Lifting her cup to her lips, she took a sip, relishing the coffee. "You know, you aren't half bad at making this." She raised her mug. "Almost as good as my uncle."

"Almost?"

"I can't see anyone surpassing him. He's got the art of brewing coffee down to a tee."

"You're really close to your uncle. Did he raise you?"

She pushed to her feet and cradled her mug between her hands as she strolled to the bay window and opened the blinds. The sun peeked over the horizon to the east, promising a clear day. "It looks like the weather will cooperate today, and the workers will be able to fix up the outside with more lights and cameras."

"And fortify the fence that surrounds the house," Slade agreed. "When I put that up, I wasn't thinking of keeping people out, only cattle and horses."

She heard the scrape of his chair across the tile floor and tensed but didn't peer his way. She didn't need to see or even hear his approach. The hairs on her nape sent small electrical signals to her brain that told her he was right behind her. His scent wrapped about her, driving away the heady aroma of coffee that drifted from her cup. "That's why another locked gate will be put up to block the road that leads to the house," she murmured, desperate to keep their conversation impersonal.

So far during the past four hours, she'd managed to divert any questions about her personal life. But Slade Caulder wasn't a man who gave up easily. Right from the beginning when they had begun to work together at three-thirty in the morning, she'd sensed a curiosity in him. About her.

"I know what you're doing, Elizabeth."

His whispered words tingled the area right below her ear. As much as she tried not to, she shivered. "What?"

"It's become obvious to me that you don't like to talk about yourself."

She whirled about, stepping away in the same motion. "And you do?" *Tell me about your wife. Why haven't you taken off your wedding ring after five years?* "I did a little checking and didn't find much about you."

"Touché. We're both cautious about trusting. But

do you blame me? Look what is happening to me and my family. What's your reason?"

Elizabeth laughed, although to her own ears it sounded shaky. She sidled away and faced the entrance into the kitchen. "I can't believe the smell of coffee didn't wake you up before now," she said to her uncle as he entered.

"I woke up at five to that smell and realized if I got up I'd get a lecture from my niece about not taking care of myself, so I went back to sleep." Joshua glanced at the table. "What have you two been doing?"

"Coming up with prospective suspects. We went through Slade's files on fired employees for the past year who live in Texas." Elizabeth went to the cabinet and took a mug, then poured her uncle a cup.

"Find anything that jumps out at you?" Joshua inhaled deeply the aroma coming from his cup. "Ah, wonderful."

Slade picked up the list they'd made. "Maybe. Here are the names in order of threat." He went on to explain Kevin Sharpe's presence on the paper. "The next one is Sam Howard. He was fired for sexual harassment of a fellow employee. He wasn't too happy about that. He was a manager going places. The third one just didn't do his job. He almost cost us a big contract."

Joshua pointed to the last name. "Why is she on the list?"

"Paula Addison stole from the company. We prosecuted her, and she went to jail. I almost didn't put her on the list since she should still be in prison, but Elizabeth thought we should check and make sure she's there."

Joshua slanted a look at her. "Good thinking. Never assume anything."

"There was another person we left off the list. Jay Wilson." Elizabeth eyed the one folder set off from the others.

"Why?" Joshua asked.

Slade fingered the lone file near his elbow. "Jay Wilson was caught passing information to the competition. He took the plans for a new software program. He denied it, but the evidence was hard to ignore. He had to be escorted out of headquarters by security. I contacted the police and pressed charges. It never came to trial, though, because he died."

"How?" Joshua sipped his coffee.

"I'm not sure."

"I'll check into it to see if there was anything suspicious about his death."

"Why?" Slade's features scrunched into bafflement. "He's dead. He can't be behind this."

"I like to check out all details." Joshua tapped the list. "I can get this to Ted, and he can have his detectives look into it."

"We thought we would do our own checking, too." Elizabeth lifted her mug and watched her uncle for his reaction. Although she'd always done some investigating on her own to help her in her position as a bodyguard, she'd never said anything to Joshua, who was a traditionalist when it came to his former job.

His eyes flared slightly. Then one eyebrow rose. "You are?"

"I can't sit by and do nothing," Slade said, drawing her uncle's attention to him. "This is *my* family. While I know the police and sheriff will do what they can, it doesn't hurt for us to do some inquiring, too. All information will be passed on."

When Joshua swung his gaze back to her, she shrugged, and he shook his head. "What kind of inquiring?"

"I'm good with a computer. There's a lot I can find out sitting right here, so you don't need to be concerned I'll go out and confront anyone. I have a family to think about." Slade stared her uncle down, making it clear by the hard set of his jaw that he wouldn't be deterred.

"Since I'll be with you, I'll pitch in, too." Joshua took his mug and walked to the bay window to check the grounds.

"Pitch in doing what?" Abbey asked from the doorway, dressed in jeans, a long-sleeved pink T-shirt and boots.

"We're looking into who could be behind what's going on." Slade's gaze traveled down his daughter's outfit. "Are you going somewhere?"

Abbey tilted her chin at a defiant angle. "I'm going riding. I've got to get some fresh air."

Slade straightened. "That isn't your call."

SIX

Out of the corner of his eye, Slade looked to Elizabeth.

Abbey shoved her hands onto her waist. "Am I gonna have to stay in the house the whole time? I'm not leaving the ranch."

"If you can give me a few minutes to change, you can show me the barn. I need to check it out anyway." Elizabeth wanted to wear something more appropriate to the barn than black slacks and a white shirt. She walked to the counter, finished the dregs of her coffee and set the mug in the sink.

"That sounds like a good idea. I'll tag along." Slade placed his cup next to hers and turned toward his daughter, his gaze snagging Elizabeth's for a few seconds. Doubt lit those pewter-colored eyes.

"It would help me as well to have a tour of the barn area and meet your cowhands." Joshua hurriedly downed his drink. "I was going to anyway today."

"You *all* are coming?" Horror highlighted Abbey's

face in an almost comical expression. "Maybe I should have made myself clear. I wanted some fresh air alone."

"Not an option. Elizabeth is with you whenever you leave this house. Inside, you can be alone, but not outside, even on the ranch." Slade strode toward his daughter and paused in front of her to wait for her to move out of the way. When she stepped to the side, he continued. "I'll meet everyone in ten minutes in the foyer. Abbey, you'll have to wait until then."

As Elizabeth passed the teenager, something in her eye made Elizabeth leery. Elizabeth took the stairs two at a time and changed into some jeans, boots, a shirt and a jacket in record time. When she arrived three minutes later in the foyer, it was empty. Hurrying outside, she caught a glimpse of the teen as she slipped through the gate closest to the barn. Elizabeth jogged toward the girl and cut the distance between them in half a minute, the whole time scanning the terrain around them.

As they neared the barn, Elizabeth placed a call to Slade and told him where they were. The second they entered through the large, open double doors, Elizabeth clasped Abbey's upper arm to still her. The young girl whirled around and jerked away, glaring at her.

"I hate this. I didn't do anything wrong. I don't

know why this is happening to me." Abbey's loud voice drew a couple of wranglers from the stalls.

A rugged-looking man in his mid-thirties wearing old jeans, a flannel shirt and a black hat and boots came out of the tack room near them. His tanned features creased into a frown. "Abbey, what's going on?"

The girl opened her mouth to say something, but instead snapped it closed and folded her arms across her chest.

"I'm Elizabeth Walker, Abbey's bodyguard." Elizabeth held out her hand to the man.

He shook it. "I'm Jake Coleman, the foreman."

"Abbey isn't used to having me with her."

"Slade filled me in on what has been going on. Me and my men will be keeping an eye out for anything unusual."

"Great." Elizabeth noticed Abbey's mouth tremble, before the girl dug her teeth into her bottom lip. When tears glistened in the teen's eyes, Elizabeth gave the foreman a smile, then rotated toward the young girl. "Why don't you show me your horse?"

A young man, probably not many years older than Abbey, who looked like a younger version of Jake, stepped completely out of the stall to the left and said, "I'll get her. She's in the pasture behind the barn."

Abbey started after the young wrangler. "I'll come with you."

"Why don't you wait here with me?" Elizabeth asked her.

"I can't even go outside right behind the barn? Where am I gonna ride Sassy?"

"Use the indoor training ring," Jake suggested from the entrance into the tack room before disappearing inside, leaving Elizabeth alone with the teenager.

Chicken, Elizabeth wanted to shout at the retreating foreman, but she couldn't blame him for escaping. The look on Abbey's face fluctuated between anger and the sense of overwhelming emotions she didn't know how to control. Her eyes still held unshed tears while she'd pressed her lips together so tightly they were a thin, hard line.

Elizabeth approached Abbey. "You have an indoor training ring? Where?" Although she was pretty sure where it was, she hoped Abbey would answer. Maybe if she got her to talk about something other than her lack of freedom, Abbey would accept the situation.

"The big building next to this one," the teen answered in a surly voice.

"That will be a great place to ride. You don't have to depend on the weather being nice."

"So bad weather and maniacs make its use necessary?" Abbey's glare strengthened into an even more furious look.

Patience. Lord, I need an extra dose of it today. "I understand from your dad you used to show horses. I haven't ridden in years, but I enjoyed it when I was a young girl." She'd been able to get away from living in a house full of strain and ride as though she raced the wind.

"Well, isn't that nice?" Abbey stared off to the side, her arms still crossed over her chest.

"Look, Abbey, we can either work together to make this situation bearable or we can be on opposite sides. The latter won't change the situation and could make it worse." Elizabeth spied an older man dressed as a wrangler come into the barn and go into the tack room. She made a note to find out who he was as soon as she could calm Abbey down.

The girl's head remained turned away, but a tear slipped down her cheek. She swiped it away and finally peered at Elizabeth. "I still see my computer screen. What did I do to someone to make them that mad at me?"

"I don't think you did anything. It's more likely your dad, but we still have to consider it might be someone who holds a grudge against you. Like Kevin Sharpe."

Abbey's face drained of its color. "Kevin? He left Dawson Academy. I haven't seen him in eight months."

"Is there anyone else who, like him, might have a reason to be mad at both you and your dad?"

"What kind of people do you think we are?" Another tear leaked from her eyes and fell on Abbey's hand as she scrubbed it across her cheek.

But before Elizabeth could explain that a person didn't have to be reasonable in their anger, Abbey pivoted and stomped toward the back entrance into the barn. The teenage wrangler led a large chestnut mare inside. Abbey grinned at the young man, saying something to him that Elizabeth couldn't hear.

She took a step forward as Joshua and Slade came into the barn. Fury chiseled Slade's features into a hard countenance. He marched to his daughter and demanded her full attention by standing between her and the mare.

"Next time I ask you to wait for us you better wait, or you'll find out what being totally grounded means. I won't let you send Elizabeth on a merry chase to find you. Do I make myself clear, young lady?"

Red blotches popped out on Abbey's cheeks. Everything from her stance to her expression screamed anger. Seconds faded into a minute before she said, "I understand perfectly."

Elizabeth approached them while Joshua hung back, surveying the barn and the young wrangler still holding the rope to the horse. Abbey spun around to pat her mare, and from Elizabeth's angle, she could see the teen's expression collapse into a combination of anger and embarrassment. She remembered back to when she was growing up and her battles with her father. This could be a difficult time for a parent and child, and with the threat to their safety added to the mix, it could become disastrous.

Abbey took the rope from the wrangler's hand. "Thanks, Brody."

"Sure." With a smile deep in his dark eyes, the young man tipped his hat, then jogged back toward the wheelbarrow to get out of the line of fire.

The older cowboy exited the tack room, pausing when he saw everyone in the barn. He shoved his brown Stetson back from his forehead to reveal a tanned face, lines of experience carved into his countenance.

Stroking her mare's neck, Abbey threw a look over her shoulder at her father. "Can I ride in the pasture near the barn?"

He shook his head. "Use the training ring for now. Too much is going on today. I want this ranch secured first."

Elizabeth panned the area and realized it would never be totally secured. Not even the White House was. The older wrangler moseyed out the double doors with a rope clasped in his hand.

Joshua came up beside Elizabeth. "I'm going

to check around outside and the training ring. I noticed the foreman in the tack room. Have you met him?"

"Yes, when I first came in here. Do you know the older man who went in there and just left? When I met a couple of the wranglers yesterday, I didn't meet him."

"That's Hank. He's not too much younger than me. I think he's sweet on Hilda."

"How in the world have you found that out so fast?"

Her uncle grinned. "I'm a good listener. I let people talk. Hank was concerned about what happened up at the main house. He kept asking how Hilda was."

"Do you know who Brody is?" She'd noticed a sly exchange of glances between Abbey and the wrangler. Was something going on there?

"He's Jake's younger brother. He's living in the bunkhouse since Jake married two months ago."

"So he works here, too."

"He does when he isn't in school. He's a senior at Dawson Academy."

"Has your partner got any background information on the employees at the ranch?" Her uncle worked with another retired police officer.

"Not much. Nothing that sends up a red flag."

"So Brody is on the list?"

"Yep. Why all the interest?"

"Just a gut feeling something may be going on between him and Abbey."

She found Brody had returned to Abbey to help her saddle her mare. Elizabeth had the feeling Abbey knew how to saddle her horse and had done it by herself before, but now she allowed the wrangler to brush the chestnut's thick coat, gliding his hand over it to check for burrs, before setting the saddle on the animal's back. Then, after cinching the strap around the mare, he gave Abbey a leg up. A dimple appeared in her cheek as she grinned and thanked him.

"Yep, Beth, I think you're right about that. But why would he be involved in what's going on?"

Elizabeth sent her uncle a sharp look. "Aren't you the one who told me never to rule out anyone?"

Joshua chuckled. "Too true."

As Joshua ambled toward the back door, Elizabeth moved toward Slade and Jake near the tack room. "I'll be with Abbey in the training ring."

"I'll go with you," Slade replied. "Where is Joshua going?"

"To check the area around the barn and the ring. He'll meet us there."

Jake spoke up. "Me and the men will help out. We'll be keeping an eye out. Anything suspicious, we'll call you." Jake ran the leather strap of a halter through his fingers.

"I know I can count on you. Jake and I go way back," he explained to Elizabeth.

"And I don't forget that." Jake hung up the halter, then thrust his hand into the pocket of his jeans and withdrew a key chain. "I'm heading into town to see about the bad feed. I'll get to the bottom of it." He started for the barn entrance.

Abbey guided Sassy toward the exit.

"Hon, hold up. We're going with you. I want to see what you've been doing lately."

Abbey came to a halt near the double doors and twisted in the saddle to peer at her father. "Why? You haven't watched me ride in ages."

"I'm here today to watch you."

"Don't feel you have to because of the threats." Abbey sat forward, turning her back on him, but she waited.

Elizabeth watched the foreman slow his pace and come to a stop just outside. A tall, blonde woman in her late twenties threw herself into Jake's embrace, kissing him on the mouth. The same lady she'd seen yesterday. His wife? "Who's that?"

"That's Cindy, Jake's wife."

Jake slung his arm around Cindy's shoulder and sauntered toward a black pickup. He opened the passenger door for his wife to get in, then rounded the front and slid behind the steering wheel.

Slade observed his foreman. "I'm glad he found someone."

"You two are long-time friends."

"From childhood. I was fortunate when he agreed to be my foreman. He's someone I can trust."

But not her. There wasn't any reason to suspect Jake, but as she told Joshua, trust no one. "What's this about bad feed?"

He began walking toward the indoor training ring next to the barn. "Part of the last batch delivered was moldy. One horse got sick yesterday. Thankfully Jake discovered it before any other horses got it."

"Who gave the feed to the horse?"

"Brody." His brow wrinkled, he slanted a look at her. "You think there's a connection between the feed and the attempts against Abbey?"

"Could be. They happened at the same time. It could be a tactic to throw you off or occupy your time."

At the door he paused and faced her. "Nothing will take my mind off protecting Abbey. Horses, I can replace. Not my daughter."

Her heartbeat reacted to his nearness. He was too close—that could rob her of clear thinking. Shutting down her emotions, she placed several feet between them, holding one side of the double doors open for Abbey to ride through. Her gaze tracked over the yard and road that ran in front of the ring. Nothing out of the ordinary. But still, someone was out there who meant to do harm to Abbey, and probably Slade, too.

The next day, Thanksgiving, Elizabeth stared out the floor-to-ceiling window in the dining room at all that Joshua and his contractors had accomplished. When money wasn't a problem, a lot could be done in a short amount of time. The old fence had been reinforced, but new posts were put in place for a taller and stronger one to go up tomorrow. Shifts of three two-man teams with guard dogs patrolled the yard.

Guards and upgraded camera systems were put on both the front gate and the second gate into the house compound. Cameras were hidden around the property and monitored by a security company twenty-four hours a day. The same with the ones in the foyer and other entrances into the house. Plans to have a safe room had been laid out and would also be started on Friday. By the time the weekend was over, this place would be like Fort Knox.

As a whole, that should make her job a little easier. At least when Abbey was in the house. Any other place and Elizabeth recognized the potential for trouble, especially because the teen hadn't accepted that Elizabeth would be glued to her side anywhere other than home.

Inhaling a steadying breath, Elizabeth spied

the first guests arriving for Thanksgiving dinner. The Colemans—Jake, Cindy and Brody. Yesterday while riding in the training ring, the young wrangler had managed to come into the building and watch Abbey ride. He'd planted himself in the shadows by the back door, but she'd seen him intently watching Abbey. The most alarming thing was that the teenage boy had a sealed juvenile record. Something had happened in Houston right before he'd come to the ranch to live with his older brother. She hadn't had a chance to talk to Slade about what Kyra had discovered from one of her contacts, but Elizabeth needed to. Until then, she'd have to keep a close eye on the eighteen-year-old, even if Jake was one of Slade's childhood friends.

She stepped away from the window and turned toward the long cherrywood dining table, set with twelve places. Her gaze immediately zeroed in on Slade, lounging against the doorjamb, watching her with a hooded expression.

He pushed away and sauntered toward her, his full attention fixed on her. His eyes still appeared tired, but he'd told her this morning he'd finally gotten some sleep. She'd always become uncomfortable when someone moved into her personal space but when Slade did so, instead of being cautious and antsy, she was charged, her pulse racing, her breathing shallow. This time was no different.

"Are you ready?"

His husky question hung in the air. She needed to tell him yes, but all she could think about were those gray eyes, smoldering steel that sliced through her defenses effortlessly.

"Of course," she finally murmured, "though I've already expressed my objection to this little gathering."

"It has been planned for weeks. Something we have done every year since we came to the ranch. My wife started the tradition. Mary has carried it on. If you think this is a big deal, you should see what happens during Christmas. How do you usually celebrate Thanksgiving?"

"If I'm not working, quietly with Joshua."

"These people are like my family. Besides, Abbey gets a kick out of helping Hilda and Mary with the dinner. That doesn't happen often since she turned fourteen. So much has changed lately. I didn't want that to, also. I actually got a smile out of Abbey this morning. Besides, the house is secure."

"Yes, but Kyra did some checking for me concerning Brody Coleman."

"Kyra? I thought Joshua was doing background checks on the people at the ranch, and he hadn't found anything so far."

"He is, but after I saw how Abbey and Brody interacted yesterday, I thought I would have Kyra look up Brody to help Joshua out."

"Interact? They know each other casually."

"It could be more than casual."

"You got that from what little you saw yesterday?"

"He goes to Dawson Academy, too. They have one class together. They may be more than casual friends. I wouldn't be doing my job if I didn't check into every possibility." Why was Slade so clueless to what was happening between his daughter and Brody? The shared glances. The longing looks each gave the other. If something wasn't going on, it could easily start at any moment.

Slade's eyebrows slashed downward. "What did you find out?"

"Brody has a juvenile record. Sealed so I don't know what he did, but the fact that he had been in trouble with the law bothers me."

A nerve in Slade's jaw twitched.

"Do you know anything about that?"

"No, but I'll find out what happened." His hard expression cemented the determination behind the force of his words.

"I need to get to the kitchen now that Joshua is letting the first guests inside." She would plant herself in the same room as Abbey and hope that Slade's belief in his friends was warranted.

Voices from the foyer drifted into the dining room. "I hear Jake. This will be a good time to find out about Brody."

As he passed her, although they didn't touch,

goose bumps spread up her arm. She rubbed it, trying to erase another physical reaction she had to his nearness. Under different circumstances, she might be attracted… Who was she kidding? She *was* attracted to him—but she wouldn't let it go any further than that. A man like Slade who was used to being in control, a man who ran a multi-million-dollar business, was off-limits to her. He was everything she avoided.

In the kitchen Abbey glanced up from making a salad. "Who's here?"

"Jake, his wife and his brother." With her back to the wall, Elizabeth stood in the large room where she could see all points of entry as well as Abbey.

The teen quickened her movements, her attention directed totally to her task. Elizabeth suspected it was because Brody had arrived, which only reinforced what she thought. They were involved or at least interested in each other.

As Slade strode into the foyer, Joshua shut the front door after allowing Jake, Cindy and Brody into the house. "I'm glad you all could make it. I didn't know if you wanted to spend Thanksgiving by yourselves this year, since it's your first one as a married couple. Here, let me take your jackets."

Jake helped Cindy out of her coat then shrugged out of his and handed them to Slade. "I can't pass up Hilda and Mary's cooking."

Cindy laughed. "I'm the first person to tell you I'm not a good cook. I'm learning, but it's gonna take some time." She grasped her husband's hand. "Time I'm happy to say Jake has given me."

After grabbing Brody's hoodie, Slade slung it over his arm. "Can I steal Jake away from you for a few minutes?"

Cindy released Jake's hand. "Yeah. Is there anything I can do to help other than actually cooking? I can chop up food or set the table."

"All the others are in the kitchen. You know the way, don't you?"

Before Cindy could reply, Brody said, "I can show her."

Slade studied the young man, a good employee who did what was asked of him, and wondered if Brody was involved with his daughter. He should know that. But then he'd have to be home more regularly to see something like that. Well, things were going to change. He had to cease working nonstop and discover what was happening in his daughter's life. He'd promised his wife he'd take care of Abbey, but he'd let his grief keep him away and had immersed himself in a job that had slowly taken over his life. No more.

"Let's go into the office," Slade said, leading the way. Jake and he had been good friends ever since they had been ten years old and Jake had stepped in to stop a bully from beating Slade up on the playground at school. He hated having to ask Jake about Brody, but this was his daughter, and he couldn't keep blinders on where she was concerned anymore.

After shutting the door, Slade faced Jake, trying to figure out how best to approach the subject of his brother. "With all that's been happening around here, Joshua and Elizabeth have done some background checks on the people on the ranch. They found something about Brody that has them concerned. I told them I would talk with you."

"They found his juvenile record."

Slade nodded. "It's sealed."

"And you want to know what he did wrong." Jake kneaded his upper arm and began pacing. "I'd hoped never to have to tell anyone here. I wanted to give Brody a clean slate, and he has done great for the two years he's been here, but I can understand your concern. My parents couldn't deal with him anymore, so I volunteered to help. He was getting involved with a gang in Houston, doing stupid things. The last one was joyriding in a stolen car." Jake paused and turned toward Slade. "I'm sorry I didn't tell you. But your offer to send him to Dawson Academy is just what he needed. A different set of friends. A different environment. His grades are good. He has plans to go to college after he graduates this year. That wouldn't have happened if he'd stayed in Houston."

Slade moved closer to his friend. "I'm satisfied. This won't go any further than this room." He held out his hand for his friend to shake.

"Thanks. I haven't even shared that with Cindy. After you gave me a second chance working here when no one else would hire me because of my drinking, I know how important it is to have a clean slate. I wanted to do the same for my little brother."

"You pulled your life together and haven't had a drink in years. I say, let's go join the others. I'm sure the other cowhands should be here soon."

"With, no doubt, their huge appetites."

"Yeah, Mary and Hilda's cooking has that effect on people." As Slade opened his office door, he took a deep breath. "I love the smell of turkey and dressing baking. I'm starved."

Jake's stomach rumbled. "I guess I am, too."

Voices coming from the dining room drew Slade and Jake. Abbey, Elizabeth and Cindy were setting the table with the good china, crystal and silver. Brody, lugging more glasses, came from the kitchen with them.

When Elizabeth peered at Slade, her inquiring gaze mesmerized him. Her dark eyelashes were long and framed the prettiest green eyes he'd seen. He worked his way toward her while an army quickly took care of the task of putting out the dishes and silverware for a big Thanksgiving dinner. Elizabeth sidled up beside him.

"Find out anything?" she asked in a whisper.

"Everything is fine. Nothing to worry about with him."

Moving back a few more steps until both he and Elizabeth were in the living room, she kept her attention trained on Abbey but said, "What was he arrested for?"

"Nothing that matters now."

"Let me decide that." She flicked her gaze to him. "You never know."

"I gave my word I would keep it confidential, but it doesn't have anything to do with what's going on here. It happened over two years ago in Houston and didn't involve my family in any way." Determined not to break his promise to Jake, Slade clenched his jaw and firmed his mouth.

Elizabeth bit back her reply. "I hope you're right. If you aren't, someone could get hurt."

"No fair, Dad. You need to help, too." Abbey glanced from Elizabeth to him, and he could see the wheels turning in her mind, trying to figure out what they had been talking about.

He surveyed the table almost completely set, even down to the bouquet of cut flowers that added a splash of color to the cream-and-gold place settings. "You all have done a great job. Where's Joshua?"

"Gus, Hank and Dan arrived. Gram didn't want

everyone standing around in the kitchen, so she sent them to the den and us in here to set the table."

"I wondered when your grandmother would kick everyone out." To Elizabeth he added, "Mary doesn't like a lot of people hanging out in the kitchen when she's creating. Sometimes she even gets rid of Hilda."

"All done," Cindy said with a wave over the tabletop. "This should showcase Mary's delicious-smelling food."

Jake's stomach gurgled his hunger. "Which I hope I can taste soon."

Cindy approached her husband and slid her arm around his waist. "Notice how important food is to Jake. Poor guy has been so patient with me."

He hugged her to him and kissed the top of her head. "It's been worth it."

"Brody, I now see why you moved to the bunk-house," Abbey said with a laugh.

The teenage boy's gaze grew warm, especially when it connected with Abbey's. "Too much mush for me."

Abbey giggled. "I'll let Gram know that we're done and will be waiting anxiously in the den."

"I'll come with you." Brody scurried around her and held the door open into the kitchen.

Elizabeth fell into step behind the pair.

Slade's hand on her arm halted her progress. As the others filed out of the room toward the den, she peered at his fingers on her. "I need to go with my client."

"Didn't you tell me the house was secure?"

She nodded.

"Then relax. This is hard enough on everyone already. Abbey should at least be able to feel safe in here. That's one of the reasons I spent so much money in the past few days doing what I could to make this a fortress."

"So you're okay with Abbey and Brody?"

"If Brody's presence at the ranch keeps my daughter here, that's fine by me. As the days go by, she isn't going to like staying near home."

"Fine. I just need to know where you stand."

A laugh came from the kitchen. Slade looked through the open door and saw Abbey tugging Brody toward the exit at the other end of the large room, telling her grandmother they would get the two extra chairs needed. "I haven't heard her laugh much lately, even before the wreck."

"Why?"

The soft light in her green eyes appealed to him, drawing him nearer. "Right after Catherine died, I had such a hard time being around my daughter. Seeing her broke my heart all over again. Abbey looks just like my wife. I started working so much that it has become a habit. I'm not sure what to do with myself except work. It took some of the pain of loss away."

Elizabeth's gaze latched onto the finger on his left hand with the wedding ring on it. When she lifted her eyes back to his face, disappointment stared back at her.

"I love my daughter, and I will readily admit I haven't been the father she's needed for the past five years. If nothing else, this maniac threatening us has shown me that. Now I just hope I have a chance to prove my love to Abbey."

"I'll pray that is the case."

Slade harrumphed. "Praying won't help."

"Why do you say that?"

"I prayed when Catherine was dying, and she died anyway. We have to solve our own problems. God doesn't have time to do that."

Elizabeth tilted her head. "You believe in the Lord, but don't think He has time for us?"

"I grew up believing there was a God. Now I don't know. He hasn't spoken to me in years."

"Maybe because you aren't listening. If you only expect one answer and you don't get that reply, that doesn't mean He didn't hear you."

"I didn't come to Him for the little things. When I finally did, it was important, something I thought was a big deal—my wife's life."

"The Lord wants to hear about all the things, little and big, you desire. But that doesn't mean He'll give you your every desire."

"Then why bother?"

Elizabeth closed the door into the kitchen and strode through the dining room to the living room. "All things are possible through God, but that doesn't mean they all will happen. I've found if I wait and listen, I'll hear what He thinks is best." Pausing at the entrance, she peered down the hallway, then toward the den. "I need to go find Abbey. I'll feel better if I know where she is."

"There." Slade tossed his head toward the den.

Abbey carried one game-table chair while Brody had the other. Slade and Elizabeth had to move to the side to allow the pair of teens to pass them. His daughter was busy telling Brody about her last play practice, when she kept forgetting her lines. The boy's rapt attention emphasized his interest in Slade's daughter. Despite what he'd said to Elizabeth, was he okay with this?

Jake was one of the few people he trusted. Jake had said Brody had turned his life around, and he was all for second chances. To Catherine, giving another a second chance was what God wanted. She'd shown him how important it was in the thirteen years they were married before she was taken from him.

Slade stared down at his wedding ring. He twirled it around his finger, remembering the day Catherine had put it on him. A lifetime ago. The day she had died, he'd felt as if his life had come to an end. But it hadn't.

He lifted his gaze to Abbey and saw his future. Then his attention strayed to Elizabeth and his gut constricted. Her beauty shone from her. The light in her eyes filled a dark place deep inside him and sparked something he'd thought was gone for good—an attraction.

SEVEN

With Joshua at Slade's ranch overseeing the work being done on the security system and Abbey holed up in her room on Friday afternoon, Elizabeth took the opportunity to go get Bosco. Her uncle liked the idea of bringing her dog to the house. That morning at breakfast even Abbey had smiled when she'd heard about Bosco. She'd asked to come with Elizabeth, but Slade had said no. That had sent his daughter storming up to her bedroom. The sound of her door slamming had reverberated through the place.

Though Bosco was at the neighbor's house, Elizabeth pulled up into Joshua's driveway first. Her uncle had done his best packing her clothes for the stay at Slade's, but there were some items he had neglected to put in her bag. She hurried to the front door and unlocked it. Inside, she quickly turned off the alarm system and headed for her bedroom. Once she gathered up the personal articles, she stuffed them into a backpack she had, then walked around the house, making sure everything was the way it should be, a habit she'd learned from her uncle.

Satisfied their possessions were in the right place, she grabbed one of Bosco's favorite toys, a red ball, and set the alarm, then left via the front door. After stashing her bag in her Trans Am, she strode to the next-door neighbor's porch and rang the bell. The sound of barking from inside made her smile. Bosco was doing what he did best. A half minute later, the teenage boy who watched Bosco for them let her into the foyer.

"Y'all back already?" he asked, munching on some potato chips from a bag he carried.

After entering the house, she knelt and greeted her dog. "No, but I've decided to take Bosco with me. I'll pay you through this weekend."

"Oh, okay. I'll get his stuff." The teen shuffled away, still eating nonstop.

Elizabeth lifted Bosco up and rubbed her face against his fur. "I missed ya, boy. We have need of your particular talents."

Bosco licked her and began wiggling in her hands.

"It looks like you're ready to go."

When the teenager came back into the foyer five minutes later, he gave her a paper sack with Bosco's toys, bowls and food. "Anytime ya need me, I'm here," he said right before he closed the front door.

She let Bosco into the passenger side of her car, then rounded the front. Her gaze strayed down the street, scoping out the area as her uncle had taught her to do. A couple strolled on the sidewalk at the far end of the block. A black Taurus sat in front of the house two down from Joshua's. Across the street, an old white Chevy truck with Ferris Plumbing on its sides was parked in the Hendersons' driveway. Nothing out of the ordinary.

Inside her Trans Am, she switched on her engine and backed out of the driveway. If traffic wasn't too bad on the return to the ranch, this trip would be no more than an hour and a half. She hated to be gone any longer than that. There were still a couple of wranglers she hadn't met, and Hilda's daughter, Kate, would be at the house by the time she arrived back.

At the end of the block as she waited at the four-way stop sign, the white Chevy truck came up behind her. Elizabeth went through the intersection. Suddenly the pickup sped around her and raced down the street. She thought about getting its license number and letting the business know about their driver speeding in a residential area. The truck whipped around the corner before she got the whole number. "Oh, well, Bosco, I'll just call the company. They should know who was working at the Hendersons'."

Bosco barked once.

Fifteen minutes later, on the twisting part of the road, her car headed up the first series of small hills, not far from Highway 156. "Halfway to the ranch. I have a girl I want you to charm."

Another yap followed that declaration.

She crested the top of the winding two-lane road on the second hill and eased her foot on the brake to slow her descent. Nothing. The Trans Am picked up speed. She pumped the brake pedal. Still nothing.

As she navigated the bends, going faster than she should, she thanked God there were no other cars on the road, especially when she veered into the other lane to make the switchback. Her Trans Am fishtailed coming out of the curve, her back left tire skating off the asphalt, dangerously close to the edge of the hill. The racing of her heart matched the speed of her vehicle careening down the incline. With a drop-off on one side and a wall of rocks on the other, she searched for any place to slow her car. One hand gripping the steering wheel to keep herself on the pavement, she eased her emergency brake up. If she could make it to the bottom, there was a stretch of flat land she could use.

As her car began to decelerate, she reached the level part. She drove along the gravel part of the shoulder. The speedometer kept dropping. But she knew there were more curves up ahead. She saw an area off the road that was a patch of brown grass and weeds leading to a dirt turnoff. She drove her vehicle toward it. Bouncing over the rougher terrain slowed her Trans Am almost to a stop. As she swerved onto the country road, she switched off her engine. She could afford to lose her steering now that she was safely off the highway.

When she came to a complete stop, she pried her fingers from the wheel, then sank against it, her forehead resting on the cold plastic. Then the shaking began, traveling from her hands up her arms and through her whole body.

The realization of how close she'd come to having a wreck shuddered through her. *Lord, thank You for being with me. Saving me.*

The scene replayed through her mind. Now the fear she'd kept suppressed blanketed her in a cold sweat. What had just happened? Joshua had had her car serviced right before she came home from her Phoenix assignment and everything had been fine. Suspicion nipped at her as she lifted her head from the steering wheel and stared out the windshield. Fumbling for her cell, she made a call to her auto service, then to Joshua.

"I need someone to come pick me up." Elizabeth tried to relax her aching muscles, laying her head against the seat cushion.

"What's wrong?" Joshua's concern immediately flowed over her, comforting her.

"My brakes went out. I'm fine. My car is even

okay. I'm having it picked up. They should be here shortly."

"Where?"

Elizabeth gave him her location, then said, "This might not be an accident. I'm going to have the auto shop check out why my brakes gave out."

"Good. I can't leave here, but I'll send someone. Be careful until then."

His warning reinforced her own thoughts. She withdrew her gun and laid it in her lap while she concentrated on the terrain around her.

"Thanks for coming to get me and waiting for the wrecker to pick up my car. I was surprised you were the one to come, Jake." Although they'd gone through the first gate and had safely arrived at the ranch, Elizabeth focused her attention on the surroundings while absently stroking Bosco, who sat in her lap.

"I was in the office with Slade when Joshua came in to tell him about what happened. I volunteered. I wanted to get to know you better. Slade hasn't shown any interest in a woman since Catherine."

Usually she was good at hiding her emotions, but since coming to the ranch she'd been having a hard time disguising her inner thoughts completely. Jake's observation about Slade's interest in her swiveled her gaze to him. "You're confusing his worry over Abbey with interest in me. We spend time together because he needs to know everything being done to protect his daughter."

Jake chuckled. "Slade and I have been friends for a long time. I know him. He's interested. I've seen the looks he gives you."

Heat flushed her face. She balled her hands, glad to see the second gate up ahead. Her ninety-minute trip had turned into three hours. Her concern for Abbey jiggled her nerves. Joshua assured her that the girl was all right, but still… What if someone had tampered with her car because they wanted her dead or at the very least too occupied fighting to keep herself alive to protect Abbey?

The interior of the pickup was warm, but chills burrowed deep into her bones. This cat-and-mouse game was taking its toll on the family. As if the person was playing with them before really doing what he wanted all along.

Jake pulled his black truck up to the front of the house. Not two seconds later the front door opened, and Slade hurried toward the pickup. Joshua came out onto the porch but hung back and scanned the yard.

"Looks like Slade is worried about you," Jake said, watching as his friend neared the passenger door. "Elizabeth, he is interested. I don't want my friend getting hurt. It took him a long time to get over Catherine."

He wasn't over her yet. He still wore his wedding

ring. But she kept those thoughts to herself and gripped the handle. "Again, thank you for the ride."

Before she had a chance to thrust open the door, Slade had pulled it toward him. "Are you really all right?"

She heard Jake's chuckle as she slid from the passenger seat, holding her dog next to her chest. "I'm fine. My car is on its way to the body shop. All's well with the world," she said in a light tone, not wanting to upset Slade any more than he already was. No reason to let him know what she suspected until she got the report back from the mechanic, a friend of Joshua's who was very good at his job.

"Don't underestimate me. I know there's a chance the person after Abbey and me may have extended it to you, too. I want to know when you hear back from your mechanic about your car."

"It wasn't a wreck. Not a scratch on my red paint. I managed to come to a stop at the bottom of the hill."

"When this is over, I'll hire you to finish giving Abbey driving lessons." Slade opened his front door and waited until she entered. When Joshua followed them into the house, Slade continued. "I'd like us to get together after dinner and go over what we know so far about the people on my list of suspects."

"Fine." Elizabeth made her way toward the stairs. "Abbey's in her bedroom?"

"Yeah." Slade crossed the foyer toward his office, down a short hallway.

At the top of the second floor, Elizabeth put Bosco down. "Remember, you need to win her over."

She rapped on the teen's door, and it was opened in seconds.

Relief flooded Abbey's face. "You're okay."

"Of course. I just went home to get Bosco." Elizabeth gestured toward her terrier. Bosco trotted into the girl's room as though he'd lived there for years.

Abbey giggled. "He's so cute." Kneeling, she let the dog stand on his hind legs, his front paws perched on her shoulder while she petted him. "Why did it take so long? I had wanted to go down to the barn to ride."

"Sorry. I had car problems. Do you want to go now?"

Abbey hopped up. "Yes, can we take Bosco with us?"

"Sure. Let me tell your dad and Joshua where we're going."

Abbey caught hold of Elizabeth's arm as she turned to leave. "Just us, please. I don't want the whole household following us down to the barn."

"So long as you ride in the training ring."

The teenage girl nodded.

"Then give me a couple of minutes and we'll go."

As she started out into the hallway, Bosco trailed behind her. Elizabeth paused in the doorway and said, "You stay here with Abbey. You two get to know each other."

With a wide grin, Abbey bent over and scooped Bosco into her arms. As Elizabeth walked away, she wondered how she could convince Slade and Joshua to stay at the house. She and Abbey needed some bonding time without the men hanging around.

That evening, cell phone to her ear, Elizabeth left her bedroom to meet with Slade and Joshua. The ride that afternoon had been encouraging to Elizabeth. Abbey had relaxed and even talked about the play she was starring in and some of her classes at school. If Abbey accepted her presence, it would make her job easier.

"I heard back from the mechanic right before dinner. The brake line was cut. What did you find out, Kyra?" She'd called her boss right after the incident with her brakes to discuss what she suspected. In all her other cases, she'd never been targeted, but now she knew she had been.

"If the line was cut, you're right that it had to have happened while your car was parked outside Joshua's house. A bold move by this person, since it was in the middle of the afternoon and you could have come out. I couldn't find anyone who remembers the couple you saw. No one else saw them. The house the black Taurus was parked outside had a friend visiting. Then I called Ferris Plumbing. They hadn't sent anyone to the Hendersons' place. The owner did say that occasionally he's discovered an employee working for himself on the side, which might be the case here. I left a message on the Hendersons' recorder for one of them to call me back. I haven't heard from anyone yet. I'll let you know when I hear back from them."

"So it could be the couple or the plumber?" Elizabeth took the stairs to the first floor, keeping her voice low. Although Abbey was working with Mary on her lines for the play in her grandmother's sitting room, she didn't want Abbey to overhear.

"Or someone you didn't see. You were in Joshua's house about ten minutes and your neighbor's house about five. Which would give someone time if he knew what he was doing. Did you see anyone following you to Joshua's?"

"No, but I wasn't looking for a tail since it was only me." She'd done her usual scan of the terrain around her and had kept track of any car that stayed right behind her for long. But she wasn't as careful as she would have been if she'd had a client with her. She was used to protecting a charge, not herself.

"The cut brakes change everything. Do you want me to get someone else?"

"No." The word was out of Elizabeth's mouth,

fast and without thought. Crossing the foyer, she started down the short hallway to Slade's office. "Anyone in this position would be in danger. I'm not leaving this job. You bring someone else in they will have to get acclimated, which will take time. What if the person used that opportunity to do something to Abbey? I'd never forgive myself. Abbey and I are reaching an understanding. That took three full days of hard work."

"I had to ask, though I agree. But it will be your call always. You have to proceed as if your life is in as much danger as Abbey's is."

Elizabeth stopped outside Slade's closed office door. "I will. Danger is part of this job. I'm the best person to be here." Because she couldn't see walking away—not when both Abbey's life and Slade's were in jeopardy.

"I'll let you know when I hear anything new."

Elizabeth clicked off her cell and stuffed it into her front jean pocket, then went into the room, expecting to see her uncle with Slade. But Slade was the only one there. "Where's Joshua?"

"He'll be here in a moment. He's talking to his partner about Jay Wilson, the man who took plans for a new software program. How's Bosco settling in?"

"I can't pry him away from Abbey. He took to her immediately, and she to him." Elizabeth settled her tired body on the soft cushion of the wing chair across from Slade's position on the couch. Until now she hadn't realized how weary she was. But the aftermath of the adrenaline rush that afternoon finally hit her.

"Which means she'll be wanting another dog after this." Stacks of additional personnel folders that he had had delivered that morning instead of next Monday covered the coffee table in front of Slade. He closed the file he had been reading and put it back on top of the pile. "I'm glad we have some time before Joshua joins us. I've decided to call Kyra and have you taken off this assignment."

The announcement stunned Elizabeth. Her mind blanked for a few seconds, as though someone had jumped her from behind, paralyzing her into inactivity. "Why?" She managed to keep her voice level, although she gripped the arms of the chair, her fingernails digging into the leather.

"I can't be responsible for something happening to you. You could have died today or been severely injured."

"What do you think a bodyguard's job description is? Danger is part of every assignment I'm on." She forced herself to ease the rigidity that held her and released her grip on the chair. Anger wouldn't make her point. Logic would. "Abbey and I have come to an understanding. Do you really have the luxury of looking for the right new bodyguard, then going through a period of adjustment? And if someone else had been in that car today, do you think they could have done any better job at controlling the situation than I did?"

"No, but—"

"I want to stay. I've never backed down from a challenge. You need to face the fact that it makes sense to keep me in place. We don't know what this person has planned. You can't afford to risk a change at this time."

With each logical reason she gave him, Slade's frown deepened until a nerve in his jawline twitched.

She leaned forward, her gaze drilling into his. "I'm good. Give me a chance."

He wrenched his look away, staring at the closed blinds over the large window in the office. Behind the slats was a wall of darkness. That wall reminded him of how he'd felt when Catherine had died. He hadn't been able to protect her. He was concerned about his ability to protect his daughter and now Elizabeth, as well.

Lord, why are You doing this? What have I done wrong?

The office door opened, and Joshua entered. Surely her uncle would agree with him, but before he could put the question to the man, Elizabeth said, "Slade wants to remove me from this assignment because I might be in danger."

Joshua took the other wing chair. "I'd advise

against it. It would be a disruption in what we've done so far. We now know that Elizabeth and I aren't safe from an attempt so we'll be prepared. Besides, I taught my niece a lot of what she knows. She's capable of dealing with this situation in a professional way."

"Every precaution has to be taken," Slade said. He could never forgive himself if something happened to Elizabeth. Being attracted to her had complicated this. He needed to shut down his feelings for her.

"Of course. She's my niece."

"Who happens to be in the same room." Elizabeth crossed her legs, her mouth a tight slit.

"Point taken," Joshua said with a chuckle. "I just got information about Jay Wilson's death. It looks like an accident when he was cleaning his gun. There were some questions—murder was considered, and so was suicide. I've got a call in to the detective who investigated the death. He's gone for Thanksgiving and won't be back until Wednesday. I'd like to get his take on what happened. I'm having a hard time believing he had an accident while awaiting trial."

"How about the others on the list?" Elizabeth bounced her leg, drawing Slade's attention. For a moment he didn't hear what Joshua was saying. Finally Slade dragged his gaze away from her and focused on Joshua.

"With Paula Addison still in prison, I think the only good suspect on that list we started with is Kevin Sharpe. His parents reported him a runaway a month ago."

"We'll need a picture of him." Elizabeth put both feet on the floor and rolled her shoulders.

"Done. I'll distribute the photo to all the security personnel at the ranch as well as your employees."

"How's the search through these files going?"

Elizabeth's question drew Slade's attention to her again. A softness in her green eyes reminded him of new, tender leaves on a tree, something he always looked forward to in the spring. "Slow. Copies are with the police. Maybe they can come up with a suspect. I feel like I'm missing something."

Elizabeth exchanged a look with Joshua. "We can help this evening, and anyone we single out, Joshua can pass on to Ted. He'll make sure attention is given to this case."

Slade scooted forward and took a stack of folders, then passed them to Elizabeth. After giving Joshua his own pile, he said, "I think I'll put a pot of coffee on. This may take a while."

"Sounds perfect to me." Elizabeth rose. "And while you are handling that, I'll go let Mary and Abbey know where I am."

She walked beside him as he left his office.

Images of what could have happened to her today taunted him as he watched her go up the staircase. At the top she glanced back at him, and his heart-beat kicked up a notch. The grin that flirted with the corners of her mouth underscored what he found so attractive about her. She had the most beautiful smile. It showed deep in her eyes and touched the cold place in his heart.

Hurrying toward the kitchen, he shook his head as though that would rid him of thoughts of the woman. Ever since he'd met her on Tuesday in Kyra's office, he hadn't been able to forget Elizabeth.

Five minutes later, he came into the foyer as Elizabeth descended the staircase, talking on her cell. Her face darkened with a frown as she listened to the caller. After she thanked Kyra for the information, she slid her phone back into her pocket. She looked up, her gaze homing in on him. The tiny lines between her eyebrows highlighted her concern.

"What's wrong?"

"The Hendersons, who live across the street from Joshua, didn't have a plumber coming to their house today. In fact, they weren't even home."

"What's that mean?"

"That the person in the Ferris Plumbing truck was probably the one who tampered with my car."

"And you didn't see him."

"No. I didn't even get a good look when he passed me on the street. The tinted glass hid a lot of him from view. I glimpsed a dark baseball cap, but that's all. It happened so fast." Elizabeth finished descending the stairs. "Kyra called a contact at the police precinct and discovered the owner had just called in one of his trucks as stolen. They haven't found it yet, but hopefully they will soon. She's having her friend check into it for any clues as to who might have stolen it. If she hears something back on that, she'll let me know."

"Wouldn't it be nice if the person left a couple of fingerprints on the steering wheel—or, better yet, lost his wallet in the truck?"

Elizabeth laughed. "You're a dreamer. I should have realized that."

"Why?" Her vanilla scent teased his senses, and it took all his concentration to focus on her answer.

"Because you started your company with a revolutionized computer chip that you came up with. You had a vision and made it a reality."

"I never thought of it that way."

"I'm a much more concrete person. I believe in facts."

At the door into his office he turned toward her. "So I won't catch you dreaming?"

"No, wasted time."

"You've never dreamed?"

"Sure, as a child. But I learned not to." She pushed the door open and entered.

Her last statement sparked more questions, but one look at Elizabeth as she spoke to her uncle made it clear Slade wouldn't get any answers.

EIGHT

"That's it for today. You all did great." Spread out before Elizabeth in the exercise room were five teenage girls from the cheerleading squad and Abbey. Sweat beaded Elizabeth's forehead, and she took the towel slung around her neck to wipe it away. "Any questions?"

"When can we do this again?" Lily, breathing hard, brushed her long brown hair away from her face.

"Yeah," several of the girls chimed in.

Elizabeth peered at Abbey. "That's your call."

"I've got play practice after school all next week. How about next Sunday afternoon after the play is over with?"

"And in the meantime, you all can practice the moves I taught you."

"I'm just glad to know what I can do if someone attacks me." Lily ambled to her bag and picked up her bottled water next to it, then took a swig.

"Me, too," Lindsay added, getting her drink.

"How many want to go riding?" Abbey asked, avoiding eye contact with Elizabeth.

Three of the girls declined because of other commitments, but Lindsay and Lily wanted to.

After the three teens grabbed their gear and left, Elizabeth pulled Abbey to the side. "I don't think it's a good idea."

"Why not? Your uncle has finished making this place like a prison. Guards are everywhere on the ranch. No one is expecting us to go riding. It wasn't planned. So what can go wrong? Today is beautiful, and I need to be outside in the fresh air."

For a few seconds her brave front fell, and Elizabeth glimpsed a scared, vulnerable young woman. "We need to run this by your dad."

"Please make him understand I need this. I haven't been out this whole holiday weekend, except to ride in the training ring. I didn't even go to church this morning. I want at least a little of my life back."

The plea in her voice hammered at Elizabeth. She knew how hard all of this was for Abbey. "School is tomorrow. You'll be going there and to play practice afterwards."

"Please talk to him about letting us ride today. We don't have to be gone long."

"Okay, I'll talk with him."

Elizabeth headed to the door. She knew how hard it was for someone to stay inside a house for days and days, especially a teenager who was used to doing a lot of activities. That was one of the reasons Joshua had expanded out from the house to secure the ranch as much as possible.

She found Slade on the couch in the den, reading some reports. She paused in the doorway, noting the tiny furrows between his eyebrows as he concentrated on what he was going over. His mouth formed a neutral slash. He jotted something down on the paper before him, then looked up.

His gray eyes brightened. "How was the tae kwon do lesson?"

"Productive."

"Good. I liked your suggestion to teach Abbey and her girlfriends how to protect themselves. The more she knows, the better this dad is going to feel even after the scumbag threatening us is caught."

Elizabeth crossed the den and sat in a chair near Slade. "Abbey wants to go riding with Lily and Lindsay. I told her I would ask you."

"I'm gathering not in the training ring."

She nodded.

"What do you think?"

Leaning forward, she rubbed her hands together. "That's a tough one. If I had my preference, she'd never leave this house, but I also know how hard that would be, especially with a headstrong teen like Abbey." Behind her she heard someone coming into the room and twisted about to see Joshua entering.

"Abbey wants to go for a ride with her friends. What do you think, Joshua?" Slade placed his report on the coffee table in front of him and rose.

"It should be okay. All points along the exterior fence are being monitored."

"Then, yes, Abbey can go, and I think I'll go along, too. A ride sounds good. I have to admit getting out of this house would be nice." He slid his gaze from Joshua to her. "How are you two on horses?"

"I was born in Texas. I learned to ride a horse before a bike," Joshua said with a grin.

"Me, too." Elizabeth pushed to her feet, actually glad they were all going on a ride.

"Then we'll meet in the foyer in fifteen." Slade strode toward the exit, a spring to his gait.

"Are you okay with this?" Joshua asked after Slade disappeared from the den.

"Yeah. I have to admit that I'm looking forward to it, too, and I know one young girl who will be ecstatic. I'd better go tell her the good news."

But when she arrived at the exercise room, Slade had just finished telling Abbey, Lily and Lindsay. The smile that graced Abbey's face wiped any apprehension away for a few seconds. Then when Abbey threw her arms around her father and he hugged her, Elizabeth felt his decision had been right. Desperate people did stupid things. This would help Abbey deal some with her curtailed life.

"Dad, you're the best. We'll be ready." Abbey spun on her heel toward her friends. "I've got some clothes you two can wear."

En masse, the teens left the exercise room. Slade turned toward Elizabeth, his expression of joy melting her heart. "I wish I had my camera to capture that smile." The distance between them shrank. "I can't believe I'm becoming as excited as my daughter. I haven't ridden in months. It'll be good to do it again."

She started toward the hallway. "You live on a beautiful ranch and you haven't ridden lately? I'd be out there every day if possible."

"Yeah, put that way it's kinda hard to believe. Working all the time has carried its price."

Elizabeth slowed her pace and looked sideways at him. "Is that regret I'm hearing in your voice?"

"When Abbey was hurt in the car wreck and I was trying to help her, all I could think about was the time I'd wasted working and not getting to know my child." He stopped at the bottom of the staircase and faced her. "You know, this situation has made me take a good, hard look at what my life has made me become."

"And what is that?"

"A workaholic living in the past." He put his foot

on the first step. "When all this is over with, I have some making up to do with my daughter."

"Why wait?"

He halted, rotating enough so that his arm brushed against her. "You're right. There's no reason. We're largely confined to the house, the ranch."

"You really are going to work here?"

"I thought I would go into the office at odd times—nothing scheduled—but mostly work from here. This past week, I've managed. I have good people in place over the different divisions of my company."

"So you're going to rely on them."

Surprise flitted across his face. "I guess I am."

"Will that be easy for you?"

"No. I've always been a hands-on employer, but I'm finding I can't do it all. Other areas of my life suffer when I totally focus on my business."

"I have a feeling your daughter will appreciate the shift." She would have if her father had given her the love she'd wanted.

"I hope I'm not too late."

She smiled. "It may not be a smooth road, but I don't think you're too late. I saw how Abbey responded in the exercise room."

The girls, all seemingly talking at the same time, came down the hall and stopped at the top of the staircase.

"You aren't ready, Dad."

He quirked a grin. "Five minutes."

She and Slade hurried up the steps and down the corridor. At the door to her room she peered at him heading toward his suite with long, purposeful strides. He turned as though he sensed her looking at him. Her heart throbbed against her ribcage. The snare of his gaze trapped her for a long moment.

The sound of laughter from the foyer broke their visual connection, and Elizabeth quickly opened her door and slipped inside the room. Leaning back, she splayed her hand over her heart, its thudding finally decreasing. But the intensity in his eyes stayed with her as she pushed away from the door and rushed to get dressed.

Slade came up behind Elizabeth in the barn as she bent over to lift the saddle. She was petite, and in order to saddle the horse, she would have to swing the saddle up over her head. Not an easy task. "Do you need help?" He hurried to take it from her.

"I can manage."

He ignored what she said and took the saddle. After swinging it over the back of the tall gelding, he fastened the cinch. When he faced Elizabeth, anger marked her expression.

"What part of 'I can manage' do you not understand?"

"I thought I was…" The fury in her eyes scorched him and erased the rest of his words from his mind.

"You thought I couldn't do it. I have before and I could have now. When I need help, I'll ask."

Who hurt her? The furious independence he'd glimpsed these past five days piqued his curiosity. Something major must have caused it. He didn't know much about her outside of her professional credentials, and he suddenly realized he wanted to know more about her. Not just because she was the woman protecting the most important person to him, but because she genuinely interested him, all on her own.

After checking to make sure her saddle was how she wanted it, she glanced over her shoulder at him, then swung around toward him. "I'm sorry. That sounded harsh, and I know you were only trying to help. But I lift weights, and I'm capable of lifting the saddle."

"I get it. You know how to take care of yourself. Were you always this way?"

"What way?" she asked innocently, but there was a mischievous glint in her eyes.

"Furiously independently and capable of taking care of yourself. I think if you were stuck on a deserted island you'd be able to find a way to get by."

"Actually, I took a survival course where they

dropped me in the middle of a desolate place, although not an island, and I had to find my way back to civilization with one bottle of water and a knife."

"How long did it take you?"

"Two days—and one of those days was cold and rainy."

"And you paid to do that?"

"Twice in the past three years. It's a challenge, but nothing beats knowing you can survive off the land."

"Remind me not to have you plan my vacation."

"Do you take any?"

He chuckled. "That's a good point. Not since my wife died. She used to force me to go, and I would gripe for the first day and then have a great time."

"You've got it bad."

"What?"

"Working all the time."

"At least my vacations aren't a test to see if I can survive off the land."

"Yeah, because you don't take any."

Amusement danced in her eyes, making the past week's events seem distant for a few minutes. His gaze zoomed in on her lips, and a constriction in his chest underscored the sight. He wanted to kiss her. That thought nearly bowled him over. He should take a step back—actually stand clear across the barn from her—but for the life of him, he couldn't move.

In the background he heard Abbey talking to Brody and Jake coming in from the pasture with Cindy. But as far as he was concerned, he and Elizabeth were the only two that existed. He tore his gaze from her mouth and trekked upward to lock on her eyes, slightly wide, all amusement gone. In its place, a gentle light warmed their depths.

"Hey, Slade, Cindy and I would like to go riding with you all."

His foreman's deep, gruff voice, filled with laughter, drenched him as though he'd dumped a bucket of freezing water over his head. Slade veiled his expression as he twisted toward Jake. Several long seconds later, he connected with the merriment in his friend's eyes, and heat rose in Slade's cheeks.

"Sure. We aren't going far. To the lake and back."

While Elizabeth led her gelding out to the back and mounted, amazingly agile and with no help, he saddled his horse.

Jake kissed Cindy. "I'll get your mare and bring her outside."

His wife smiled. "Thanks, honey. It'll be good to practice riding some more."

Slade swung his attention away from the happily married couple and walked Ace of Spades, his black gelding, to where everyone was gathering to ride.

Seeing Jake and Cindy together brought forward how much he missed having that kind of relationship with a woman. The casual touch or kiss, the silent communication conveyed in a look.

As he swung up into the saddle, the sunlight of an unusually warm November afternoon caught the gold of his wedding band. He needed to accept Catherine's death and move on or he would probably never give his daughter the attention she needed.

But as he fell in beside Elizabeth, he knew that wasn't the only reason he wanted to move on. The woman next to him interested him. He intended to discover who had hurt her. Who had chiseled that independent streak into her heart? And would he be the one who could help her heal?

An hour and a half later, when Elizabeth returned to the main house with Slade, Abbey and Joshua, she saw stacks of plastic containers scattered in the foyer and overflowing into the den and living room. Cinnamon-scented candles perfumed the air along with the aroma of baking cookies. Strains of "Joy to the World" echoed through the house, thanks to a state-of-the-art sound system.

Abbey covered her mouth with her hand. "Oh, no, Gram has struck."

Through the clear plastic of the crates, Elizabeth saw lots of red and green objects. Christmas decorations. Maybe she could escape to her room until the festivities were finished. Judging from the grin splitting Joshua's face, he would be fine with the decorating and could certainly protect both Abbey and Slade.

"This has been the first day without all the contractors and workers around lately," Mary said as she came into the entry hall. "So are you all ready to decorate the house for Christmas?"

The cheerful words nudged memories of childhood holidays to the forefront of Elizabeth's mind. She didn't want to experience them again. She'd always been thankful Bryan didn't care much for Christmas except to get presents. He didn't even want to put up a tree. And then once she'd become a Christian, she'd focused on the reason for Christmas, not everything else that went with it. Celebrating with Joshua had been a quiet affair because he'd known how she felt.

As Mary took the tops off of several bins full of decorations, Elizabeth didn't think the holidays would be a quiet time in the Caulder household.

"Does this bother you?" Slade whispered close to her ear.

His breath on her neck rippled down her length. "Why do you ask that?"

"You went pale when you saw all this." He gestured toward the plastic containers.

"There's a lot here."

"I have a big house, and that isn't it."

She angled her head toward him, hoping she'd wiped all expression from her face, but when she glimpsed the interest in his eyes, their color like molten silver, her mind went blank, and she could tell from the flare in his gaze that her expression didn't go neutral. She glanced toward the staircase.

Slade inched even closer. "Thinking of escaping upstairs?"

Intensity vibrated between them. She did want to escape, not just because of the decorating, but because she didn't like the feelings Slade's nearness generated in her. As though she couldn't control her responses to him. As though they were more than employer/employee. As though there weren't someone out there wanting to harm Abbey and possibly him—even her.

The doorbell rang. Elizabeth flinched, not expecting the sound. Her hand went to her holster. Joshua started forward to answer the door, but Mary moved faster, reaching for the knob first. Joshua's hand covered hers, and Mary blushed.

"We're going to need some help since we're behind schedule, so I invited Jake, Cindy and Brody to supper and to help get us ready for Christmas." Mary swung the door wide, not giving Joshua time to check the peephole.

As the Colemans entered, Joshua murmured to Mary, "Always check who's at the door even if you're expecting someone."

Mary stabbed him with a look. "You've got this place locked down tighter than a cookie in a toddler's fist."

Elizabeth smiled as she heard her uncle reply, "Nothing is one hundred percent secure, and I'm being paid to protect you all, so let me do my job."

The sound of Mary's huff wafted to Elizabeth as she turned away. Her gaze collided with Slade's amused one.

He leaned closer, his scent of the outdoors encasing her in memories of the afternoon riding with him. "Now you'll have to stay since Brody is here."

"I thought you'd cleared him."

"As Joshua just pointed out, you can't be too cautious."

"You're enjoying yourself, aren't you?" Mere inches separated their mouths, and Elizabeth couldn't stop thinking about that.

As Mary began giving out bins and directions on what to do, Slade whispered, "What about the holidays bothers you?"

"The commercial aspects of Christmas," she said quickly, using her pat statement for whenever anyone asked her.

Slade studied her face for a long moment. "I'm sure that generic answer is part of it, but that's not all."

"We could use your help, Slade, Elizabeth." Mary pointed to two containers at her feet. "These go in the den. Brody has gone with Jake to get the tree from storage. After supper I thought we would put the ornaments on the tree, but we've got a lot to do before that."

"You use a fake tree?" Elizabeth asked as she hefted her bin and walked toward the den.

"According to Mary, a fake tree can stay up longer and isn't as messy." He stopped just outside the entrance into the room. "But really, she's allergic to pine. Catherine was, too, so we have always had an artificial one."

"That makes sense if you're into all this." Elizabeth moved through the doorway first, the whole time conscious of Slade's attention on her. This was going to be a long evening.

When supper was finished and most of the garlands and other decorations were up, Slade helped Mary by carrying a tray of hot chocolate into the den while she brought her oatmeal-raisin cookies. The past few hours as he'd helped to get the house ready for the Christmas holiday, he'd managed mostly to forget someone had targeted his daughter, even gone after Elizabeth because she was protecting

Abbey. But then he would catch sight of Joshua or Elizabeth, wearing their guns in holsters at their waists, and the whole past week would crash down upon him.

Mary set the goodies on the game table. "Are you all ready to tackle the tree? We've got tons of ornaments to put up."

Elizabeth's eyes grew round as she took in the multiple containers of Christmas balls. "I know you have a large tree, but you're gonna need at least one or two more for all these." She swept her arm across her body.

"Which reminds me, I bought a new tree for the living room. Our ornament collection keeps growing each year. Elizabeth is right. This one—" Mary flipped her hand toward the ten-foot artificial pine standing in the corner near the fireplace "—won't hold them all anymore. Jake, Brody, can you go get the box in the garage and put that one together in the living room in front of the large picture window?"

"Yep," Jake said and sauntered out of the den with his brother.

Cindy ambled toward the game table, took a deep breath and said, "This looks and smells delicious. Jake has raved about your hot chocolate on more than one occasion. I can't wait to try it."

Mary picked up a large mug with chocolate syrup

drizzled over a thick mound of whipped cream. "Here, enjoy. Take a cookie, too."

"I will. Thanks." Jake's wife snatched up several treats and took the drink from Mary.

Mary passed out the hot chocolate. "You might let it cool a little while we get started."

"Where do we start?" Elizabeth said to Slade, putting her mug down on a coaster on the coffee table next to her.

"Pick a box and just begin putting up the decorations."

"No special place you want certain ones?"

"No. Wherever there's a place for one. As you'll gather, when we're through, you'll hardly be able to see the tree."

Abbey knelt by a box with her name scribbled on top. Carefully she lifted the first ornament out.

"Catherine made those for her, giving her a couple each year. She always puts them on the tree first."

Elizabeth faced Slade. "Ah, should we wait until she finishes?"

"No, we'd be here an extra hour if we did. You can help me put on the ones that Abbey made."

"Are you sure? Don't you want to put them on by yourself?"

He laughed. "You haven't seen the amount." He gestured toward two boxes.

"All of those?"

"Yep, she got into it, more than her mother. I miss Abbey making me one. She hasn't done it in several years."

After Mary drank some of her drink, Cindy took a tentative sip of her hot chocolate, then another one before she stooped next to a container with their collection of expensive ornaments given to the family over the years.

Elizabeth looked where he was staring. "Those are beautiful."

"Yeah, but they go on last if we have enough room. I've gotten a lot of them from suppliers, people who want my business. Family ornaments come first." Slade watched Cindy pick up a stunning glass ball decorated with jewels and crystals.

Cindy held it up, her gaze fastening to his. "I've never seen such a gorgeous ornament." She started to put the ball back in the container when she flinched, her face screwing up in pain.

Mary rushed toward the trash can in the corner at the same time as Cindy rose to her feet, her face going white. His mother-in-law fell short of making it as she began to throw up. Cindy bent over, the glass ball slipping from her fingers, as she also was sick. The sound of the ornament shattering propelled Slade into action. Elizabeth was already halfway to Cindy.

He moved toward Mary. Two people sick at the same time. What was going on? With all that had happened lately, a sense of foreboding inundated Slade as he assisted Mary toward the hallway.

Hilda emerged from Mary's bedroom.

Flanked by Slade and Abbey, Elizabeth pushed off the wall outside the older woman's suite. "How is she?"

Hilda glanced toward the closed door. "Fine, now. She's not sure what happened. She's tired and going to rest."

"Can I go see her?" Abbey asked, worry furrowing her forehead.

"Just a moment. She may already be asleep."

"Thanks, Hilda, for helping Mary." While his daughter went in to see her grandmother, Slade grabbed Elizabeth's hand. "We need to talk."

As he descended the staircase to the first floor, his fingers still around hers, he slanted a look toward her. "Could what happened in the den be connected to the other threats and attacks?"

Joshua, waiting at the bottom of the steps, answered. "I intend to find out. I collected a sample of the hot chocolate they drank—actually, a little from all the mugs, as well as other things we ate and drank. But since none of us got sick but Mary and Cindy, I'm pretty sure whatever did this was in the hot chocolate. I'll have it checked for poison, but it makes me think of syrup of ipecac. I knew someone who was bulimic and used that. Happens quickly. Usually a person feels okay afterwards, just maybe a little lethargic."

Slade's cell rang, and he quickly answered it. "So she's all right, then." He listened, then said, "Good. Thanks, Jake, for letting me know. Tell Cindy she doesn't need to worry about the ornament. It can be replaced." When he hung up, he said to Joshua and Elizabeth, "Cindy was more worried about breaking the expensive decoration than the fact that she threw up. I need answers. Fast."

"It's a holiday weekend, but I can call in a favor and get the samples analyzed quickly. We should have some idea what got into the drink by tomorrow. I'm calling my partner and having him come pick up the samples." Joshua walked away from them as he withdrew his phone.

"How did this happen?" Pacing, Slade plowed his fingers through his hair.

"A good possibility is that the pantry was tampered with when the person broke into the house."

Slade stopped and spun toward her. "Then we need to throw out all the food that was open. I can't take the chance something else has been doctored."

"Let's wait until we get the lab results back."

Slade glanced up the stairs. "How's Gram?"

Abbey came down the steps. "She made me

promise we would finish decorating the tree. I told her we would."

"It's not the same without her," Slade said.

"She's coming down in a little while and told me she expected the tree at least half completed by then." Abbey moved toward the den, but before disappearing inside the room, she peered back at her dad and Elizabeth. "Are you two coming? We need to get Joshua and Hilda, too. I don't know how she thinks we can get it done with so few people."

When Abbey vanished into the den, Elizabeth shook her head. "Wouldn't it be easier to pay someone to decorate the house?"

"Don't ask that question in front of Mary or Abbey. I did once, and believe me, I never will again." Slade clasped her arm and tugged her down the hallway. "Come on. This will be fun."

After the incident with Mary and Cindy getting sick, and the rest of the evening spent decorating the house for Christmas, exhaustion wrapped about Elizabeth. No matter how hard she tried not to think of her childhood, she felt deluged with memories. Standing in the doorway into the den where the ten-foot artificial pine stood, she remembered a time when she had put ornaments on her family tree. Everything had to be placed in a certain spot, calculated by her father. And no homemade ornaments or balls that he considered inferior could be displayed. Perfection, according to her father's standard, was important even with something like holiday decorations.

Elizabeth searched out the loaded tree set up in the corner of the den a few feet from the fireplace. Earlier, lights had blazed from the tree, illuminating the whole room. Now in the shadows, she couldn't see the ornaments, but she wouldn't forget them anytime soon. Most of them were homemade. Each of them had a story behind it—where it came from, why it was important, who gave it to the family. And as they were put on the tree wherever anyone wanted, the story was recalled either by Abbey, Slade or Mary, who had been able to join them halfway through decorating the pine.

Again she could see Abbey climbing the tall ladder to place the star at the top. Tears clouded the teen's eyes as Mary talked about how long it took for Catherine to craft the glittering star. Elizabeth chanced a glance toward Slade as he watched his daughter secure it on the top limb. As if he knew she was looking at him, his gaze bound with hers.

The vulnerability she'd expected to see in him with the rush of memories concerning his wife wasn't visible. The corners of his eyes crinkled, and the smile he sent her blazed a path through her, much like the Christmas lights did through the den.

Pivoting away from the doorway, Elizabeth headed toward the pool, where she'd been going when she'd paused at the entrance. She needed to exercise—long and hard. The pool enclosure had a bank of windows across the back with skylights in the ceiling. The security lamps from outside illuminated the pool in dapples of lights. After she removed her terry cloth cover-up, she slipped into the water and began her laps.

Thirty minutes later, winded, she swam to the side and hoisted herself out of the pool, then sat on the edge with her feet dangling in the water. She tried to take in all that had happened in the past week. First the wreck, then the break-in and the cut brake line on her car. Now it might be that the person behind all this had put something in the food to make people in the household sick. Was it poison, a mild one that didn't kill but heightened the fear already in place? Or, was it what Joshua suspected, syrup of ipecac? She hoped they had some answers tomorrow. At least they should be able to learn what had happened. The "when" would be more difficult to discern. And if it was put in the food at the time of the break-in, what else had they not found yet that could hurt someone?

Standing, she dried off and donned her cover-up, checking her pocket for her weapon. A sound behind her drew her around to stare at Slade silhouetted in the entrance, dressed in jeans and a sweatshirt. Silence accompanied his trek across the tiles to where she was. He hovered over her, his expression hidden in the shadows, but energy poured off him as though he were a live wire. The air thickened with the quiet. Her pulse throbbed against her eardrums.

His fingers curled around hers, and he tugged her closer—dangerously close. "I couldn't sleep, either," he finally murmured, breaking the silence. "And then I saw the door open and thought Abbey might be swimming. She's done that sometimes when she's upset."

"What makes you think I couldn't sleep?" Breathlessness attacked Elizabeth's lungs, and her words came out in a raspy whisper.

"Well, let me see." His mouth tipped up in a lopsided grin. "It's two o'clock in the morning. Most people are asleep by that time, especially if they have to get up tomorrow and go to school at seven."

She shivered. "Oh, that makes me think of high school, and I'd just as soon not repeat that time."

"Just so you know." He bent close to her ear and continued in a hushed voice. "You are going to a high school tomorrow."

His teasing tone coupled with the caress of his breath along her cheek caused another quiver that had nothing to do with bad memories of high school. She needed space or she might throw herself at him and demand he kiss her. He lifted his hand to brush wet hair back from her face. The gleam of his wedding ring caught the light.

Reality brought her back to the moment and the fact that she was a bodyguard. She stepped away. "I don't think standing in front of these windows is the best place for you. They aren't bullet resistant yet."

"How about over there?" He indicated an alcove with chaise lounges, hidden from any prying eyes outside.

"That would be much better. I know there are guards roaming the yard and you're probably safe, but I wouldn't be doing my job if I didn't point that out."

He latched onto her hand and pulled her with him toward the alcove. "Then that cinches it. Since Joshua is asleep, I may need protecting."

A laugh escaped her throat. "I doubt it."

"But you said you can't be too sure of anything." He released her hand and gestured toward the chaise lounges. "Let's talk. I need to unwind before I can get any sleep. Decorating can be hard work."

"The kind Mary demands."

"See? That's probably why you couldn't sleep. You're tense."

Yeah, she was tense, but it wasn't from the decorating—not really. The journey into her past along with this man's presence wasn't doing anything to help her relax. "I'd better go."

She started to turn away when he said, "Please stay."

His request held a wealth of meaning that had nothing to do with being in a dangerous place.

When she didn't move to leave, he inched closer and drew her toward a chair. "I don't want to be alone right now, especially after what happened with Mary and Cindy this evening. It reconfirmed how susceptible we are."

She had known that because of the type of job she had. If it wasn't for the Lord, she wouldn't get out of bed in the morning. Life was a series of risks people had to navigate through. *Jesus is the light that shows us the way.*

"Please, Elizabeth."

The vulnerability in his appeal was her undoing. She couldn't deny him his request, although in her heart she knew how emotionally risky it was. She swung back toward him and was surprised at how close he was. "For a few minutes."

He eased down in his chair and lounged back. "How was your swim?"

"I have to admit I could get used to swimming after a long, hard day. There's something about it that makes you forget everything else."

"Then you should use the pool again tomorrow

evening. I figure after school tomorrow you'll need to relax."

She put her feet up, rested her head back against the chaise lounge and closed her eyes, relishing the sound of the waterfall at the other end of the pool. "Yeah, it wasn't that long ago that I went to high school. That's one time I wouldn't like to repeat."

"Why?"

Her tension heightened with his question. She popped one eye open and looked at him in the dim lighting. "Because I was picked on and my life was generally made unbearable by a group of girls who didn't like how I dressed or walked or talked or did anything." The words tumbled from her mouth as though they had a will of their own. Except for once when she'd first come to live with her uncle, she hadn't told another soul about the nightmare her high school days had been—not her parents or Bryan. And now she had confided in Slade—a man she had known less than a week. But instead of panicking at her admission to him, she managed to shake off the taut grip the question had on her.

"I was a nerd in high school," Slade replied. "Always fidgeting with a computer. When someone needed help with theirs, they brought it to me to fix. Otherwise they didn't say much to me."

"So I guess we agree that high school stunk for us."

"Except for the last year. I met Catherine, and she

changed everything. She gave me the confidence I needed to believe in myself. Well, that and meeting Jake. Not too many people picked on me because he was my friend. People didn't want to cross him. He was the captain of the football team and on the wrestling team, not to mention he was already riding bulls in the rodeo."

"No wonder you and Jake are good friends."

"I'm glad he's finally happy. His fiancée walked out on him a week before they were going to get married. After that, he never got too serious until Cindy." He sat up straight. "So what's your story? What's the real reason you don't like the holidays?"

"You don't buy my answer about them being too commercial?"

"Oh, I think they are and I believe you do, too, but that isn't the real reason horror filled your expression when you saw all those decorations." He placed his feet on the tile floor and leaned toward her.

"Memories of growing up in a household with a strict father who never showed me any kind of love have made me avoid anything having to do with Christmas. I never knew what the real meaning of the season was until I became a Christian, but I still have a hard time not remembering how it was as a child."

"Whereas I had fond memories of the holidays with my wife and daughter, but after Catherine died, I found it hard to keep up the same amount of enthusiasm even for Abbey. Mary has done her best to celebrate Christmas in this house like Catherine did, and slowly my mother-in-law has drawn me into the festivities."

"Maybe you're finally ready to move on."

"But you aren't? I hear a lot of anger toward your father in your voice. I may not go to church much anymore, but I do know one of the things the Lord wants us to do is forgive others."

This conversation was getting too personal. She swung her legs to the floor, determined to move the focus to him—not her. "Why don't you go to church anymore?"

He lifted his shoulder in a shrug, his knee only inches from hers. "I was angry at God for not saving Catherine."

"Are you still angry?" she asked, realizing she was still mad at her father. She hadn't forgiven him and wasn't sure she could.

Cocking his head to the side, he stared ahead for a long moment. "Not like I was. Anger takes a lot of energy, and right now all I want to do is keep my daughter alive."

The love that sounded in his voice when he talked about Abbey tempted her to forget she didn't want to get involved with a man, especially one who thought she needed protecting, coddling. She couldn't shake the conversation on Friday about him wanting to fire her and get someone else to watch over Abbey—all because the person behind the threats had expanded to include her. She couldn't have another man in her life who didn't respect her ability to take care of herself.

"Talk about energy, I think the laps I swam has zapped mine. I'm going to try and sleep now." She stood, needing to end their conversation before she told him more than she already had.

Not a second later he rose, facing her. Reaching toward her, he funneled his fingers through her wet hair. "Thanks for listening to me." With each word he eased closer.

His silky voice, with a slight Texan drawl, liquefied any defenses she tried to assemble as he brought his head down toward hers.

NINE

Slade brushed his lips over Elizabeth's—once, twice before he settled his mouth on hers and drew her against him, his hands sliding down her back. The touch of her against him awakened feelings in him that he'd thought died with his wife. All he wanted to do was hold Elizabeth in his embrace and protect her from any harm.

He deepened the kiss, and for a brief time the loneliness of the past five years vanished. The taste of her on his lips seared into his memory, threatening to never let go. He shouldn't pursue this, he knew the risk to him if he did, but he couldn't help himself. He needed more in his life. It was as though he'd been starving for years and suddenly a banquet was spread before him. But what would happen if he gave in? He cared about her, and yet he didn't know if he had it in him to love her as he should. He'd given Catherine everything. Was anything left for him to give to another woman?

The realization that he wasn't ready for anything

beyond friendship brought him to his senses. He stepped back, ending the kiss abruptly. "I'm sorry. I shouldn't have done that." And yet deep in his heart he wanted to deny the words he'd said to her. He wasn't sorry, not when she made him feel good—alive.

She didn't say anything for a long moment. His heart beat rapidly against his chest. *What were you thinking,* an inner voice shouted over and over.

Finally her features set in a bland expression. She pivoted and strode toward the door.

"Elizabeth, wait."

She took three more steps before she halted. Her stiff bearing conveyed anger, and he couldn't leave it like that.

At the door, he leaned around her and opened it. "I'm sorry. I—"

"Please don't say that again. For the record, I'm not sorry you kissed me. For the past few days I think you and I have been dancing around the issue of this attraction for each other, but now we know it won't go any further." She sounded as calm as he wished his pulse rate was. Cool as the winter wind that blew outside.

She made her way down the hallway toward the staircase, not glancing at him. He kept pace with her, intending to explain his actions whether she wanted to hear or not. When she planted her foot on the second floor landing, she peered at him and said, "Good night."

But he wasn't going to be dismissed that easily. He clasped her hand and stopped her escape. "I had one love in my life, my wife. I'm a bit rusty with all of this."

One eyebrow arched. "What? With kissing or making sure the woman understands no strings attached?"

He opened his mouth to answer her, but she pulled her hand from his grasp and placed two fingers over his lips. "Don't say anything. I understand. My life is totally different from yours. This isn't where I belong—not once the threat is gone. So don't worry. And don't apologize. Now if you'll excuse me, I'm tired and need some sleep." Her touch slipped from his mouth, and she quickly strode toward her bedroom.

There was a part of him that wanted to go after her. Make her understand. But understand what? Even *he* didn't understand what was happening between them.

The doorbell chimed as Elizabeth rushed into the den for a strategy meeting Monday evening. After spending all day at school with Abbey, she was exhausted but hadn't wanted to be left out. Sheriff McCain was joining her, Joshua and Slade. The test results on the hot chocolate had come back.

The chocolate drizzled on the whipped cream had been doctored with syrup of ipecac, almost as if it were a childish prank.

"Sheriff, can I get you something to drink?" Mary asked as she showed him into the room.

"No, I'm good. Thanks." He took the last chair at the game table and waited until Slade's mother-in-law left before continuing. "Have you found anything else in the house?"

Joshua shook his head. "We did a thorough search today from top to bottom for any kind of listening device or anything else that looked suspicious."

"Not to mention we threw out all the food that had been opened. Hilda restocked the pantry." Slade drummed his fingers against the tabletop.

Elizabeth sensed how upset he still was that Joshua had insisted Hilda have a security guard go with her to the store—not because Joshua thought the housekeeper was in danger but because he wanted an impartial person with Hilda. The implication hadn't been missed by Slade or the housekeeper. According to Joshua, Slade had been adamant that Hilda had nothing to do with what was going on at the ranch, whereas the older woman had accepted the escort with graciousness.

"Why don't you leave town?" The sheriff laid a manila envelope down.

"Then have him follow us and hassle us in an unknown place? No, I'm not going to give him that chance. Nor let him lie low until we finally come back, and then start all over again. We need to find him before he succeeds in killing someone." The tapping of Slade's fingers on the table increased.

"Okay. I needed to ask. My office and the Dallas police have talked with Kevin Sharpe's friends. No one knows where the boy is, or at least that's what they're claiming. The lab reports on the plumbing truck they found Sunday have come back, and all the fingerprints taken were accounted for. But the steering wheel was wiped clean as well as the door handle and gearshift. We've done some checking on the list of suspects you've given us, Slade, and the only one that looks promising is Paula Addison."

Elizabeth sat forward. "I thought she was still in prison."

"She is, but she's been having weekly visits by her boyfriend, an ex-con who was convicted of assault. We're trying to track him down for questioning, but he's disappeared. He hasn't been at his apartment in Silver Chase for several days." He opened the envelope and withdrew a photo. "This is Dwayne Olsen. Have any of you seen him anywhere?"

Elizabeth stared at the picture, trying to imagine a baseball cap pulled down low, but no matter how much she wished she'd gotten a clear view of the driver of the plumbing truck, she hadn't, not with the tinted windows and the speed the man was going. "I don't think I've seen him."

Joshua and Slade both shook their heads.

"I'll leave this with you. Show it to your ranch hands. Let the security guards see it, too."

Slade slid the photo toward him. "I appreciate it."

Sheriff McCain stood and pushed in his chair. "Oh, you mentioned to me that Sam Howard took a job overseas. I discovered today he was fired from that job two weeks ago and has returned to the U.S. He's living in Oklahoma City with his mother."

Slade rose and shook the sheriff's hand, thanking him. After the lawman left, Slade settled back into his chair, elbows on the table as he formed a steeple with his fingers. "He's only a few hours away from here. Close enough to cause trouble. Okay, so the list of the most likely suspects at this time is Kevin Sharpe, Sam Howard and Paula Addison's boyfriend."

Although Elizabeth wanted to add all the cowhands and even Hilda and her daughter, just because they had access, she wouldn't. Having access didn't make a person guilty. There needed to be a motive—something behind what was going on. From what she'd seen, his employees at the ranch respected and liked Slade. "Speaking of Paula's boyfriend makes me think we should take a look at people close to the list of suspects."

"That's a good suggestion, since we're running out of suspects from DDI." Joshua took the photo of Dwayne from Slade. "We'll need a recent one of Sam Howard now, since he's nearby."

"The one in his personnel folder is good. Last I saw him, he hadn't changed in the five years since it was taken." Slade began drumming his fingers again. "We aren't narrowing this list down at all. We just keep adding to it, and now we're adding relatives."

Joshua pushed away from the table and to his feet. "We don't want to miss anything."

"No, I can't afford that."

The doorbell chimed. Joshua swiveled his attention toward the hallway. "No one was expected. I'd better get that."

Elizabeth trailed her uncle, with Slade a few steps behind her. Joshua kept his hand near his holster as he checked the peephole. His stiff stance relaxed a little as Abbey came bounding down the staircase with Bosco yapping behind her. Joshua opened the door to let Brody in.

"I'm glad you could come help me." Abbey hugged a notepad and textbook to her chest. "Let's go into the den to work."

Slade stepped to the side, and Brody passed him. But when his daughter started to follow, he moved into her path. "It's late."

A pout tugged at the corners of Abbey's mouth while Bosco sat at her feet waiting. "I'm having trouble with this Algebra II assignment. Brody is good in math. He offered to help me."

"I could have."

"I never know when you'll be busy."

Her statement hit the mark. "He can stay an hour." Slade clamped his mouth shut and sidestepped to let her by with Bosco trotting behind his newfound friend.

Abbey wouldn't be able to put her off that easily. Elizabeth marched after the teenage girl. Although she'd planned on going up to bed early, Elizabeth didn't trust Brody. She wouldn't be far from Abbey whether the girl liked it or not.

Abbey threw a glance over her shoulder and planted herself in the doorway into the den. "Please don't stay in the same room as us," she said in voice that held none of her earlier pertinacity. "I promise you, nothing is gonna happen." Shadows clouded her eyes. "Please."

"I won't go far."

Abbey didn't move right away but stared at Elizabeth, then she murmured, "Fine," spun around and headed across the room to the game table to sit next to Brody.

Elizabeth backed away and planted herself against the wall across from the entrance into the den. Slade walked down the hallway, took her hand and pulled her toward the staircase.

"What do you think you're doing?" She tried to yank away from him, but he increased his grip.

"Making myself and you comfortable." He plopped down on the second step and patted it. "Join me. You can see the doorway from here."

"Aren't you concerned about Brody at all?"

"Not as the person behind this, but I was a teenage boy once and I certainly know what's going through that young man's mind. So yes, as a father I am concerned, but if I smother Abbey any more than she's already smothered, she'll pull something. This is an easy concession to give her." He settled his elbows on his thighs and leaned forward, lacing his fingers together. "Besides, this gives us a chance to talk. I think you've been avoiding me since you got home with Abbey."

"I saw you at dinner and a while ago in the den," she said, though she had been staying away from him. When she saw him, she thought of their kiss the night before. She thought of her reaction to it, then the disappointment when he'd pulled away from her. She should have been the one to end the kiss, but she'd given in to her feelings.

"Maybe we should talk about last night."

"Why?" She angled around so she could better keep an eye on the entrance into the den.

"You left upset. That's not what I wanted."

"What did you want?"

He cradled her face with his large, strong hands. "To kiss you again."

"Don't!" Panic tangled itself in that one word. She shot to her feet and stood in front of the staircase.

"You're as conflicted as I am." Rising, he invaded her personal space. "I know all the reasons you and I shouldn't be attracted to each other in here—" he tapped his temple "—but in here—" he placed his hand over his heart "—I want to ignore all common sense and pursue what you make me feel."

She started around him. "I'll be by the den door."

"Elizabeth."

A couple of feet away, she peered back.

He rubbed his thumb over his wedding ring, then he slipped it off his finger and put it in his pocket.

"What are you doing?" Again that panic was back in her voice, and she clenched her teeth to keep from revealing any more of her emotions.

"Finally putting my past behind me. When are you going to?"

"I don't know what you mean."

He shook his head. "Yeah, you do. You had a lousy childhood, and you're letting it control who you are today. You want to keep people at arm's length. Forgive your father. Move on."

Tears she hadn't shed in five years welled up from

her depths. She wouldn't cry. Not again. "It wasn't just my father."

"Who else hurt you?"

"My ex-husband."

He took a step toward her.

She held up her hand. "Don't come any closer. This discussion is over. I have a job to do." Whirling around, she hurried down the hallway and took up a place across from the entrance into the den.

As she folded her arms over her chest, she glimpsed Slade climbing the stairs. He'd taken off his wedding ring. She couldn't get the picture of him slipping it off from her mind. For just a few seconds when he had, a seed of hope embedded itself in her heart. Then she remembered her failed marriage and realized she could never make herself vulnerable like that again.

Late Friday afternoon, Elizabeth stood in the wings of the stage, watching Abbey rehearse the lead in the play, about a young woman trying to find her way home for Christmas and running into all kinds of obstacles. Abbey was good. The story reflected some of Elizabeth's journey as she pieced her life together after Bryan had left her. Like Laura, the character in the play, Elizabeth had struggled with her self-esteem, thinking she had deserved everything that had happened to her—

even the mugging when she'd been searching for a job after the divorce.

This past week witnessing the rehearsals after school had left her raw each night when she'd returned to the ranch. The extra long days at Abbey's school had given Elizabeth the excuse to hole herself in her room when Abbey went to hers after dinner. Because every time she saw Slade, thoughts of his kiss, of him taking off his wedding ring, plagued her with feelings she couldn't have.

She wouldn't go there again. She couldn't lose herself as she had with Bryan—actually had all her life until five years ago. Uncle Joshua had shown her the way to stand on her own two feet. She couldn't let herself forget that.

As the dress rehearsal wrapped up, Abbey stepped back to let the cast stream off the stage. Abbey came off last after talking with the director, Mr. Greenly. There would be only one performance, tomorrow evening, Saturday. The cast and crew had been invited back to the ranch after the play for a late celebration. It had been planned for a month, and Slade had hated to cancel something that meant so much to Abbey. Joshua had hired a few extra guards to cover the grounds and house while Elizabeth wouldn't let Abbey out of her sight.

She wasn't looking forward to tomorrow evening. It would be a long night. One she would be glad to see over.

"What did ya think?" Abbey said, her excited voice in contrast to the tired lines on her face.

The past several nights Elizabeth had heard Abbey up until late—sometimes practicing her lines, other times receiving texts and calls until all hours. "You're gonna be good. Laura is a perfect role for you."

The teen beamed. "I get her. Her parents didn't understand her. Couldn't relate to her. She felt stifled by them."

"Until she left and discovered the world."

"Well, I haven't done that yet." Abbey weaved her way through the props and cast to the dressing room she shared with the other females in the play.

"You will."

"Not soon enough for me. There's so much I want to do. I wish I was graduating from high school like Brody is this year."

"You like him, don't ya?" She didn't need the teen to answer her—the evidence spoke for itself. Every lunch this past week, Abbey and Brody had eaten together. Several times during the school day they'd met in the hall and talked for a few minutes until they had to get to class—usually with Abbey jogging to make it on time.

"Well, he's cute. Sweet. And he's great with a horse. I think he's gonna follow in his brother's footsteps with the rodeo." Abbey removed her costume and changed back into her jeans and blazer. "Let's go. I can remove my makeup at home."

Elizabeth called the security guard parked outside to let him know that they were coming out. He would pull the car around to the side door, which was only five feet away from the curb. Once they left the auditorium the press of people thinned. Only two other kids were in the corridor that led to the east exit. Elizabeth kept an eye on the two teenage boys down at the end of the hall, at the same time aware of her surroundings and anything that might be unusual.

The two teens turned down another hallway at the other end, leaving Elizabeth and Abbey totally alone. Elizabeth's gaze swept the empty passageway, where only some of the lights were on. Three more feet and she and Abbey would be outside in the armored plated SUV and heading home. After she stopped Abbey so she could check the exterior, Elizabeth pushed through the door and scanned the dark parking lot, where there were a half a dozen vehicles.

Where was the guard with the car?

The hairs on the back of her neck stood up as though an electric shock had passed through her body. She stepped back into the building and pointed toward the far wall, away from the glass in the doors. "Stay there." Then she retrieved her cell and made a call to the security guard. "Where are you?"

He snorted. "Some moron cut me off. I'm almost there. Twenty seconds."

"Did you get the license number of the car?"

"Yep. I'm here."

Elizabeth clicked off and stuffed her phone back in her pocket. "Let's go." She stepped outside first and checked the area, then hurried Abbey to the SUV with bulletproof glass.

Once inside the vehicle Elizabeth didn't stop her vigil but kept panning the traffic around them. She called in the license number to Joshua to run down, then said to the driver, "Make sure our route is different from yesterday."

Abbey angled around to see the school disappearing from her view. "What happened back there?"

"Probably nothing, but someone cut off Kurt when he was coming to pick us up."

"Why's that a big deal? People do it all the time."

"As I said, probably nothing, but I'm paid to be suspicious about everything."

"I'd hate living my life not trusting anyone."

Abbey's comment made Elizabeth pause. When she was working, not trusting anyone was part of her job, but it didn't stop when she was off the clock. She lived her life like that, but it wasn't her job that caused it. Her past relationships with her father and

Bryan had driven that point home to her. Now, she protected herself, stayed safe—but the cost was never feeling close to anyone. Was that really how she wanted to live her life? "Are your friends still coming over on Sunday afternoon for another tae kwon do lesson?"

"Yeah, Lily even wants to go riding again. She and Lindsay have been my best friends for years."

Elizabeth's life wasn't conducive to having many friends, and there were times she missed that. "Maybe we can do both."

"I haven't gotten to ride all week with play practice right after school. Brody told me Sassy misses me." Abbey leaned her head back against the cushion. "I think I'll text Brody to bring Sassy in from the pasture and put her in her stall. After dinner I'll go down to see her and hopefully ride her in the morning. It'll help me forget the play is tomorrow evening."

"We'll see."

Abbey threw her a frown. "I shouldn't have to run everything by you."

"I know this is hard for you."

"Has anyone ever curtailed your activities when you didn't do anything wrong?"

"Yes," Elizabeth murmured, then wished she could snatch the word back.

"Who?"

She didn't want to have this discussion but

Abbey's gaze drilled into her, demanding an answer. "My father. I didn't date until after I graduated from high school. He told me that was for my protection. He rarely let me go over to a friend's house unless their parents were friends of his. My day usually consisted of going to school, then home. I didn't do many extracurricular activities." She wouldn't get into the fact that she'd married a man like her father who had to control her every move.

"Oh. At least Dad never did that until now."

"And you know why he's doing it. He loves you and wants to make sure you're safe."

"Like your father?"

"He's nothing like my father," Elizabeth said with such force even she was surprised by the vehement tone.

"Then tell me why my father is always working. I've seen more of him in the last couple of weeks than in months. His usual routine is to go to work early and come home late."

"Why don't you ask him?"

Abbey's eyes grew round. She stared at Elizabeth for a long moment, then turned her head and looked out the window.

For the rest of the ride to the ranch silence ruled, and Elizabeth was glad. Why was she being forced to talk about her father after all these years? *What are You trying to get me to do, Lord?*

She didn't have an answer to that question twenty

minutes later as they pulled up to the main house at the ranch. Both Elizabeth and Kurt got out first and looked around before she waved for Abbey to exit the SUV. The teen slung her backpack over one shoulder and rushed to the front door, which opened before she reached it.

When Elizabeth entered a few seconds behind her, both Slade and Joshua stood to the side as Abbey took the stairs to the second floor two at a time.

"Did anything else happen?" Slade asked, watching his daughter vanish down the upstairs hallway.

"No, the ride here was uneventful." If you called telling Abbey more than she intended uneventful. "Did you find out who the car belonged to?" Elizabeth asked Joshua, troubled by Slade's assessing gaze as if he were delving into the secret places in her heart.

"Yes. The man doesn't appear to be connected at all to Slade or Abbey. He's an electrician but has never done any work here or at DDI. So he was probably just an irate driver hurrying to get home."

Elizabeth exhaled a deep breath. "Good. I don't think Abbey would be too happy if she couldn't do the play tomorrow night and have the cast party here."

"I thought you were against the party," Slade said

as Joshua proceeded to lock down the house, a routine he did each night when everyone was home.

"I am. If I had my way, I'd put my client in a locked room reinforced with steel with no windows and no visitors."

"Solitary confinement. That would go over well with Abbey."

"She could text or chat on her cell."

"Oh, then that would make everything better." A twinkle gleamed in his eyes.

"Fair warning. She wants to go to the barn and see Sassy tonight after dinner."

"I don't see why we can't take a walk down there if she wants. None of the guards patrolling the ranch have seen anything out of the ordinary in the past week."

"So you think the guy has given up?"

"Maybe." He peered at her. "Okay, probably not, but I can wish."

"He's just waiting for you to let down your guard. Tomorrow night would be a good time for him to strike."

"Everyone attending the party has been checked out. Joshua has doubled the detail for the event. Since Mary has had to cancel our Christmas open house, she's using this as a holiday celebration."

"So everyone is happy." Elizabeth started for the stairs, needing a little down time before their late dinner.

"What happened? Did Abbey give you a hard time? Or did something go wrong at school that I should know about?"

"No, nothing happened at school. Abbey still isn't thrilled to have me trail her around, but her friends seem to accept me. In fact, I think another friend is going to join us on Sunday for the self-defense class."

"So the pain I see in your eyes is from nothing?"

How did this man get to be so perceptive? Most people she'd worked for never bothered to ask questions about her personal life, her feelings. Often she'd felt invisible in their homes, which had been fine with her. But here she wasn't invisible, and she was having a hard down shutting down her emotions. "We talked a little bit about feeling confined. She challenged me when I told her I knew how she felt. I ended up telling her a little about my relationship with my father."

"What did she say to that?"

"She shared with me some of your relationship with her."

"Ouch."

"Why do you say that?" She needed to keep the focus of the conversation on him, not her.

"Our relationship hasn't been good lately, and I'm to blame for that."

"Have you told her recently that you love her?"

As a teen she'd kept hoping to hear those words from her father. He never said them.

Slade thought for a moment. "No, not nearly enough."

"That would be a start." Elizabeth mounted the first step, still needing that down time to piece together the armor she wore to keep herself apart from others. Obviously she wasn't doing a good job if Slade could read her like he did.

When he followed her up the stairs, she sent him a questioning look.

"There's no better time than now to talk to Abbey. Mary said dinner will be—" he looked at his watch "—in twenty minutes."

At his daughter's room, he rapped on the door and waited for her to open it. Elizabeth went into her bedroom, but Abbey didn't appear. After knocking again, he thought a moment about trying the handle. What if something was wrong? Yes, the house was secure, but...

He grabbed for the knob at the same time Abbey pulled the door open. He quickly dropped his hand to his side.

She frowned. "I was in the bathroom."

Censure in her voice challenged his intentions for being there. "Can I come in?"

"It's your house."

"It's yours, too," he said as he moved into the middle of the room.

"Not really. If I had a choice, I would be living closer to town, nearer my friends."

"I thought you loved this ranch."

The frown still firmly fixed on her expression, she plopped down on her bed and sat cross-legged on it. "When I was little, I did. There isn't much to do here."

"You love to ride."

She shrugged. "It's okay."

When did this all change? What had he been doing? Working. "Why didn't you say anything to me?"

"Because you and Mom loved it here. And now that she's gone…" Abbey swallowed hard. "I never see you."

He took a step toward her. "Honey, I'm sorry. We used to be so close, and I pushed you away after Mom died."

She shut her eyes for a long moment. When she reestablished visual contact, tears pooled in her gaze. "Why? I needed you."

A huge knot in his throat prevented him from replying for a long moment. He swallowed several times. "I know I let you down. I was too caught up in my own grief to see anyone else's. I thought if I worked hard I could forget and everything would be all right. It isn't."

He sat on the bed, wanting to draw his daughter into his arms, but she scooted back against the headboard, curling her legs up against her chest and clasping them to her. The barrier might as well be a high, thick, stone wall separating them.

"If you want to move closer to town when this is all over, we will," he finally said, not sure how to mend the damage his grief had caused in their relationship.

"But you love the ranch. It has always been your dream."

"But my dreams have changed since I grew up. What I want more than anything now is for us to be a family again."

The doubt in her eyes stared back at him. "I want to go down to the barn after dinner to see Sassy. Can I?"

Had she heard a word he said? "Sure. I need to get out of the house."

"Alone."

That one word pierced his heart. Nothing he'd said had meant anything to her. "You can't without Elizabeth, at least."

She pinched her lips together, laid her chin on her knees and somehow managed to tug her legs even closer to her chest. "Fine. But just her. I don't need an entourage everywhere I go."

"I'm not an entourage."

"If you go, then Joshua does."

He shoved to his feet. "Okay. Dinner is about ready."

"I'm not hungry. Lily had a sandwich at play practice. I ate half of that."

He'd obviously handled this all wrong. How could he fix this? At his work when there was a problem, he came up with a solution and executed it. He strode to the door, opened it and turned back. With the side of her head on her knees, she stared away from him.

"I love you, Abbey. That will never change." He waited a moment, hoping to get some kind of reaction from her, if only a look. Nothing.

He slipped out of her bedroom and quietly closed the door. Had he just made the situation worse? He didn't know the first thing about raising a teenage girl. A boy he could have related to, since he'd been one once, but Abbey was an enigma.

Like Elizabeth, he thought with a sigh. His urge to protect the ones he cared about extended to her, but she was determined to need no one. Was it possible to get beneath that tough facade she presented to the world?

TEN

Standing backstage watching the play Saturday night, Elizabeth was counting down the minutes until the performance was over and she could get Abbey out of the auditorium. Only five more minutes. On stage, Abbey's character Laura fell into the arms of her parents, tears running down her face as they welcomed her back home on Christmas eve. The tree behind the trio shone bright with lights and red and green glittering balls against the backdrop of a den, fake bookcases painted on the plywood that included a mantel and blazing fire.

Elizabeth peeked into the audience and found Slade recording the show. He sat in the front row with Mary, Hilda and her daughter, Kate, Jake, Cindy, Brody and Joshua. They had all come back to the dressing room right before the play to wish Abbey the best. The tension between Abbey and Slade still charged the air as it had all week. Obviously Slade's talk with his daughter hadn't gone well last night.

When the performance ended, the audience came to its feet, the applause deafening. The cast members took their bows in order of importance then left the stage until Abbey, as the lead, was the last one remaining. The people clapped even louder. A huge grin plastered Slade's face. Brody gave a wolf whistle. Abbey made one bow, then another, as the crowd greeted her with more acclaim. She backed up as though to leave, but her director from the other side of the stage gestured for her to stay and enjoy the ovation.

Then a young girl walked out on stage and gave Abbey two large bouquets of red roses. Tears in her eyes, she made one final bow and started for the wing where Elizabeth was waiting for her. When Abbey was a few yards away, a brilliant light flash and a popping sound reverberated through the auditorium. Elizabeth charged forward, glimpsing out of the corner of her eye the scenery of the den start to sway.

Elizabeth seized Abbey, the bouquets of roses scattering everywhere, and threw her toward the wings as the large piece of plywood came crashing down. Elizabeth dove after the teen. The edge of the plywood clipped the back of Elizabeth's right boot, nearly sending her to her knees. Dust flew up. The thundering noise from the scenery impacting with the floor shuddered through Elizabeth like an earthquake.

She pushed forward. She had to get to Abbey and get them out of there. Coughs racked her as she reached Abbey, who was clutching the curtain. Paralyzed, the teen stared at the stage where she'd been only seconds before.

Suddenly on each side of the auditorium near the middle, hissing sounds filled the stunned silence of the audience. Smoke billowed and roiled upward. Screams of panic overruled all common sense.

A woman shouted, "Fire," as the director came out with a microphone. The request to "Please exit in an orderly fashion" was ignored by most of the crowd.

Was it a real fire or just a smoke bomb? Even if it was relatively harmless, Elizabeth had to get Abbey out of there fast. The exits behind the stage were the only option. "Let's go." Elizabeth grabbed the girl's arm and started forward.

Abbey kept her fingers tightly locked around the dark maroon velvet of the curtain. Elizabeth pried the teen's grasp loose. She latched on to the girl as they surged through the crowd rushing toward the exits.

Pandemonium continued to reign all around Elizabeth. Frightened actors ran over each other trying to get out. She held Abbey's arm even tighter and kept panning the area backstage. The press of bodies pinned Slade's daughter to her. The left exit was too dangerous with almost all the cast and crew trying to get through it.

"What happened?" Abbey shouted over the noise of chaos.

"Don't know. Just keep going. We'll meet your dad and Joshua at the appointed place by the south doors to the school." The one they had arranged earlier in case they were ever separated. "Do not leave my side."

Elizabeth's gaze riveted to the other exit door that led to the long hallway, near the drama classroom, that ran behind the stage area. She redirected Abbey toward that exit, constantly on alert for anyone who wasn't in the play. Ten feet away the lights flickered and the sprinklers came on. Darkness shrouded them, the sounds of screaming piercing the air.

Joshua followed on Slade's heels, taking up the rear of their small party as they threaded their way through the crowd jamming the aisles and exits at the back of the auditorium. "We'll head for the south doors."

An hour before coming to the play Joshua and Elizabeth had discussed where to meet if something happened and they got split up, but Slade had hoped this evening wouldn't come down to them executing the emergency plan. He glanced to each side of the auditorium. A cloud of smoke and dust wafted toward the ceiling and snaked among the rows, working its way toward the middle. Slade held Mary's arm, trying to keep her close in the mass of people all trying to get out of the auditorium.

If Elizabeth hadn't grabbed Abbey and pushed her out of the way, his daughter could have been trapped under the thick piece of scenery, now lying flat. The boom it made still rang through his mind. Abbey's frozen stance for a precious few seconds before Elizabeth pushed her to safety would stay in his thoughts for a long time.

Was Abbey all right? Elizabeth? "I can't do this. Let's go backstage and try to catch up with them. We can use one of the exits back there."

Joshua blocked his way. "No. We need to get out. We don't know what caused that small explosion that brought down the scenery. Or this smoke."

"Exactly. They could be in danger."

"Trust Elizabeth. She'll get Abbey out safely. My job is to get you out in one piece." Joshua tried to herd Slade in the right direction.

Slade stood his ground, grasping Mary's arm tighter than he intended. He thrust his face into the older man's. "I'm going."

Joshua's eyes glinted fire. "You have more than Abbey to think about." His attention swept to Mary, then back to Slade. "Elizabeth knows what she's doing, and I've called Captain Dickerson. The police are on the way."

"This person is obviously willing to hurt innocent people to get to us."

"My point exactly, and standing here arguing about it makes you an open target that much longer." Joshua's gaze slid to Mary again. "Or others."

Mary shook loose of his hold. "Do what you need to, Slade. I can take care of myself. Jake and Brody are right in front of us."

That was all he needed. Slade plunged into the crowd right behind him and hurried toward the stage, aware of Joshua behind him.

Slade made it to the steps when the lights fluttered off and on. Then off.

Pitch-blackness surrounded Elizabeth as water from the sprinklers drenched them. The panicky screams of others trying to escape heightened the sense of danger. She tightened her grip on Abbey. "Stay close."

"I'm scared."

The whimper in the teenage girl's voice toughened Elizabeth's resolve to get them out in one piece. Recalling the way this area backstage was set up, she remembered the costume closet two feet to her left, the only door along that wall. There was only one way in. "Let's go over here," she whispered close to Abbey's ear. If it was dark for them, then it probably was for whoever had put this chaotic mess in motion. "We'll go into the costume closet.

Trying to get out of here in the dark would be too dangerous." And she didn't want to use her penlight to illuminate their location in case someone was watching and waiting.

She realized staying could be dangerous, too, but she could protect Abbey better in a stationary location with only one entrance. And she'd been in the costume closet and knew its layout. It would be unlocked because of the play. When she felt the wall, she groped until she found the knob and turned it. The creaking of the door as she opened it sent a cringe through Elizabeth.

She went in first, pulling Abbey behind her, and felt to the right where she remembered some historical-looking gowns hanging on a rack. The soft feel of velvet grazed her fingertips. She withdrew her penlight and flicked it on. "I want you to stand over here among the costumes." After Abbey positioned herself behind the row of dresses, Elizabeth arranged them to hide her, then clicked off the small flashlight. She didn't want anyone to see light from under the door. "Don't come out no matter what unless I tell you to. Okay?"

"Yes, but—"

"Abbey, no buts. I'm going to be at the door. No one will get in here without coming through me."

"Okay." Abbey's voice squeaked.

Elizabeth planted herself at the door to the side, ready to pounce on anyone who came through it.

Lord, please get the lights back on. With one hand on her holster, she withdrew her cell and called Joshua, shielding the phone's soft glow.

Right behind Slade on the steps leading to the stage, Joshua pulled out his ringing phone. The light illuminated a small area around him and Slade. Others still in the auditorium were using any means they could—from lighters to cells to penlights—to brighten the dark interior.

"Joshua, where are you and Slade?"

"Heading backstage. You two okay? Outside?"

Slade halted and turned back toward Joshua. "Is that Elizabeth?"

Joshua nodded.

"We're in the costume—hold it. Someone's trying to get in here."

"Elizabeth?" All Joshua heard was muffled sounds as though she'd stuffed her cell in her pocket. "Do you have any idea where the costume closet is?"

"Why? What's wrong?" Helplessness roughened Slade's voice.

"Elizabeth and Abbey are holed up in it, and someone's trying to get inside."

In the dim light Slade's expression toughened into a fierce look that chilled even Joshua. "I know where it is. Let's go."

* * *

The costume closet door opened slowly, and someone felt around the wall near where Elizabeth was plastered against the bricks. She braced herself for contact and slowly lifted her Glock from its holster.

"This isn't the way out," a young girl said.

"We're lost," another teenager announced somewhere behind the girl. "My cell's in the dressing room. I can't see a thing."

"No, this is the costume closet. Follow me. I know the way out." The girl shut the door and the students' voices faded.

"Elizabeth?"

"I'm still here." She heard sirens in the distance and retrieved her cell.

"What's going on?" Abbey asked. "All I remember is a flash of light, a pop and then you're pushing me toward the curtain. Is the guy after me here?"

Good question. "I don't know, so I'm assuming the worst."

"The guy *is* here?"

"Yep." She put her phone up to her ear. "Joshua, you there?"

"We're coming to get you."

"Where are you?"

"It looks like…"

Beneath the door a stream of light poured into the closet as the sprinklers shut off. Elizabeth fumbled for the handle and cracked the door open. She blinked at the brightness assaulting her eyes. Through some of the props she spied Slade and Joshua coming toward her. Relief trembled down her until she realized they still weren't safe. Although she could still hear the sirens, the police weren't there yet, and they needed to get out of the building and into the safety of the bulletproof SUV.

"I called to have the car at the south door. Let's go." Joshua motioned toward the exit along the back of the stage area.

Elizabeth ducked back into the costume closet and said, "Abbey, we need to leave."

For a moment, nothing. Alarmed, Elizabeth hurried to where Abbey was behind the rack of dresses. She parted the gowns. The teen stood frozen, her eyes large, her skin pale beneath the stage makeup that had run down her face from the sprinklers.

"Abbey?" Elizabeth touched her cold hand.

Slade's daughter blinked her eyes. "Is it safe now?"

Elizabeth debated whether to tell her the truth or not. Fear held Abbey immobile and Elizabeth wanted her to leave, but she wouldn't lie to the girl. She needed Abbey to trust her in all situations. "We'll be safe when we get outside to the SUV. Ready?"

Ten seconds passed, then finally Abbey took one step before she froze again. Elizabeth grasped the girl's clammy hand, hoping to convey some of her warmth to Abbey, and guided the teen toward the door. Abbey's teeth chattered, and her body trembled.

When Slade saw his daughter, he folded her against him and murmured, "You're okay. I won't let anything happen to you."

"We need to leave now." Joshua strode toward the door.

With a nod of his head, he indicated to Elizabeth to take up the rear, sandwiching Slade and Abbey between them. After checking the long hallway, Joshua waved them forward, and they quickly traversed the length. At the intersection with the main corridor Joshua peeked around the corner, his hand on the weapon at his waist. Elizabeth turned around and faced the way they had come. A movement caught her attention. Tense, putting herself between Slade and Abbey, she put her hand on her Glock.

Jake poked his head out of the exit, saw them and grinned. "We've been searching for y'all." He emerged from the doorway with Brody and a security guard.

"Where's everyone else?" Slade came around Elizabeth.

"They're at the car with the other guard. We got worried." Jake and the others covered the distance between them. "The police have arrived. The sprinklers took care of the smoke in the auditorium. There was no fire."

"Then come on." Joshua started down the corridor that led to the front of the auditorium near the south doors.

Elizabeth took up her position at the back. Brody flanked Abbey's left side while Slade was at her right.

The teenage boy and Slade exchanged looks before Brody said to Abbey, "You weren't hurt, were you?"

Abbey, tears filling her eyes, shook her head.

Slade slid his arm around his daughter's shoulder. His jaw set in a fierce expression as he, too, searched his surroundings for anything unusual.

In three minutes they were at the SUV in the south parking lot. People milled around outside, waiting to find out what had happened in the auditorium. Elizabeth rushed Abbey and Slade into the armored car, joining Mary and Hilda already situated in the back.

"Where's your daughter?" Elizabeth asked Hilda.

"Kate left earlier to go to the ranch to set things up for the party."

"We're not having the party." Slade pulled Abbey to him, angry determination darkening his eyes.

"Dad—"

"No. We can celebrate as a family quietly, but

no guests. Not after what happened. On the way home, I'll make a few calls, but I suspect a lot of the cast is scattered." He snapped his mouth closed and stared forward.

Elizabeth pulled back from the door and closed it, glancing around for Joshua.

"I'll find Cindy, and we'll follow you back to the ranch." Jake turned and searched the area, then waved to Cindy, who stood in the middle of the gathering crowd. He and Brody ambled toward her.

Joshua made his way to the armored SUV and climbed inside the front while Elizabeth slid in next to Abbey. "Go. Let's get back to the ranch."

Tension hung in the air as thick as the dust and smoke from the small explosive and smoke bombs. Abbey sat with her shoulders hunched and her arms hugged against her chest. Elizabeth realized how differently this whole night might have ended if Abbey hadn't rushed her steps off the stage and been close to the wing when the scenery fell. A second later, she might not have been able to get the girl out of the way in time.

Slade finished up a phone conversation, his gaze latching onto Elizabeth's. "This incident changes everything. Abbey, you won't be able to leave the ranch until we catch this person. And I promise you, we'll find him."

Left unsaid but clear by the clenched teeth and

hard lines of his face was that Slade would make sure the person paid for what had been done to his family.

Abbey started crying. She turned to Elizabeth and buried herself against her, sobbing. Elizabeth clasped the young girl against her and murmured, "You're safe now." But in the back of her mind, she knew none of them were truly safe. This wasn't over yet.

Later that night, Elizabeth checked the deserted pool room, a stream of moonlight streaking across the calm water. The house was finally quiet after the guests from the ranch had left. The planned cast party had turned into a quiet family Christmas party. Abbey was subdued and hardly said a word all evening except to Brody or the friends who called to make sure she was all right. She broke down and cried on the phone to Lily and Lindsay, especially when they said their parents didn't want them at the ranch until there were no more threats. They canceled the tae kwon do lesson for Sunday.

When Elizabeth had walked her to her room a few minutes ago, Abbey had still been concerned her friends would be mad at her because of what happened at the end of the play. She never thought that the person would do something so openly in front of so many people who had nothing to do with what was going on.

Elizabeth strode toward the den. She'd assured the teen that her friends understood and didn't blame her. But nothing she said really consoled Abbey. Exhausted, the young girl closed her bedroom door as though she were being locked into a prison cell and couldn't receive any visitors.

Entering the room, Elizabeth immediately saw the blaze going strong in the fireplace. Had someone added another log? Suddenly she sensed she wasn't alone. Whirling about, she spied Slade staring out the newly bulletproof bay window that overlooked the backyard. His hands stuffed into his pants pockets, he hung his head, his shoulders slumping.

She started to leave, sensing the despair that reached out to her and lured her toward him. She had to resist the draw or she would lose herself. Slade was strong, overpowering at times. She couldn't care about someone who could threaten who she was. She never wanted to experience another relationship like she'd had with Bryan.

"Please stay." He rotated toward her, the rawness in his eyes melting all resistance in her. "I don't want to be alone with my thoughts right now. They aren't very Christian at the moment."

"You're thinking of the person who caused this evening's catastrophe."

It wasn't a question, but Slade nodded anyway. "I never realized the depth of his hatred, to do that to all those people who had nothing to do with this. Thankfully, the evacuation progressed pretty smoothly, or there could have been a lot of injuries." Bleak eyes stared at her. "What did I do wrong to cause that kind of loathing? I've been standing here going over the list of suspects we're concentrating on, and I can't see any of them doing this."

"I've seen all kind of reasons for people to come after others. A few have been petty misunderstandings that have been blown out of proportion. I can't even begin to tell you what the thinking is behind these attacks."

"It feels like he's toying with me. Showing me he's in control of my life and Abbey's." He combed both hands through his hair. "And frankly, he is. I'm now holed up here. Abbey can't even go to school. I'm not going to let Mary leave here, either. She might be targeted next. I have armed patrols covering my ranch. If I didn't know better, I would think I'm a third-world dictator whose countrymen hate him and want to see him dead."

The softness of the leather cushions beckoned to her after the long, tiring day. Elizabeth moved to the couch and eased down onto it. She didn't think she could stand another moment and not fall over. She had finally come down from the adrenaline overload she'd had earlier at the auditorium.

"I actually was a bodyguard for twin girls of a wealthy Central American businessman. He wasn't the leader of the country but he was the man who really pulled all the strings, and some rebels didn't like the ones he pulled."

"What happened?"

"Eventually the rebels were rounded up, put on trial and went to prison. But his daughters were sent to an exclusive European school where security was tight. I was just filling in until the school year started."

"How old were they?" Slade took the seat next to her on the couch.

"Eight."

"Eight! And they were going to a boarding school? What a shame."

"They didn't want to leave their papa, but he wasn't going to take the chance someone would take up the rebels' cause and come after his children to get to him. He could afford the school, and he *couldn't* afford the risk."

"Are you telling me because I'm rich this is the way I need to live from now on?" He gestured toward the bullet-resistant window.

"No, but you can't take security for granted. You did before this. Someone may not be mad at you but your company and its product. That occurred with another client I had. The only reason the culprit was caught was that she made a bold, risky move against my client."

"Is that what I need to do? Put myself in danger to catch this person?"

"No, I could never recommend that to a client. Too many things can go wrong when you try to trap the perpetrator. Don't even think that." The thought of him as a human target constricted her stomach with pain. "But even when all of this is over, danger will still exist. There's always going to be someone who might want to hurt you. All you can do is take precautions and be prepared."

He rested his head back on the cushion. "Did you notice the silent treatment I got from Abbey tonight when everyone was here trying to pretend nothing was wrong?"

"Kinda hard to miss. She's scared and angry at the same time."

"I know how that feels. I feel the same way."

All her common sense told her not to lay her hand on his arm nearest her, but she couldn't stop herself. He was hurting, and she hated seeing him that way. "You're not alone. We'll here to help. Maybe the police will find something at the school. Some clue. Joshua will talk with Captain Dickerson tomorrow and see."

"How did he get backstage to plant the explosive device that caused the scenery to fall? Was it on a timer, or was he in the audience and used a remote to set it off? And what was set off in the auditorium?"

"Probably smoke bombs. We need to let the police do their job while we concentrate on keeping you,

Abbey and Mary safe. But if the intent was to hurt Abbey, then I think the person was there watching and used a remote to detonate the device." Beneath her palm she felt Slade shudder. "Or he was long gone and only wanted to show you how easy it was to get to you and Abbey."

"I've got the feeling he was in the audience, taking pleasure in seeing everything going down. The panic, the near miss with Abbey and you."

"That's what I think, too."

Slade hunched forward, his elbows on his thighs, and scrubbed his hands down his face. "I don't know how you do your job." He slanted his gaze toward her. "You go from one intense situation to another. And through all this, you've remained calm, even though you've been caught up in this person's schemes. He could have killed you last week. For that matter, you could have been hurt tonight. Why do you do it?"

"I'm helping people."

He shook his head. "That's not it. Oh, I'm sure that's part of it, but there's something else that motivates you. You can help people a lot of ways, but you put your life on the line in every job."

She scooted back against the arm of the couch, drawing her legs up against her chest and clasping them. "I do it because I never want children or women to feel like I did."

He straightened, his eyebrows slashing down. "How?"

"Trapped in a situation I didn't know how to get out of."

"By your father?"

"Partially, but he mostly laid the groundwork for Bryan, my ex-husband. He conditioned me to think it was normal to be put down every day, that I was worthless. Bryan spent our marriage keeping me subjected to him."

"He abused you?" Anger carved deeper lines into Slade's face.

"He never harmed me physically, but verbally he tried to destroy me. He only continued what my father had started, and if he hadn't divorced me, I don't know if I would have had the strength to find my way out of that relationship. The day my husband left me for a twenty-year-old woman was the best day of my life, but I didn't know it at the time. I'd hit rock bottom. My uncle and the Lord helped me find my way back."

He moved closer to her, putting his hand on her knees. "I'm so sorry. That experience is what led you to become a bodyguard?"

"No. I was mugged and badly beaten. That experience made me determined to never be a victim again. Once I learned the tools and tricks to protect myself, I wanted to help others by keeping them from being victimized, especially the children.

Anyone who preys on children is a monster." Tears she'd held at bay for years, since she'd been mugged, deluged her, clogging her throat, welling into her eyes. One dripped onto her bottom lashes and rolled down her cheek.

Slade leaned closer and rubbed his thumb across her face, wiping the tear away. "All I know is I'm glad Abbey has you watching her back. I never thought this person would go to such lengths to get to me, or I wouldn't have let Abbey participate in the play. I knew how much it meant to her and all the hard work she'd put into it."

"We still don't know if you're the primary target."

"He came after you."

"Because I guard Abbey."

"Someone else would have replaced you if you were hurt, so why come after you? To send me a message. That no matter what I do, he'll get to me. Look at the syrup of ipecac incident. Another taunt. He had no way of knowing who would drink it. Abbey doesn't care that much for chocolate, but I do—"

Elizabeth put her feet on the floor and stood. "Why did he only put it in the chocolate syrup?"

"I don't know why. You can't put it in dry food? Most people like chocolate?"

Digging her teeth into her bottom lip, Elizabeth began pacing. "True, I love chocolate, but there are other things I like, too. I think the person knows you, has been around you and possibly your family."

"Or has a way of finding out about us? What if those bugs that Joshua found had been there for a while?"

Elizabeth halted and rotated toward him. "That's a definite possibility. The person has taken his time, planned this out. I could see him gathering information about you before moving forward with his intentions."

"What are they? To harm me or Abbey or both of us? To kidnap Abbey?"

"Probably not, or why did he announce his presence to us? It certainly is harder to kidnap her now, especially after this evening."

"Then he wants to—harm us, but first he wants to make our lives miserable." Slade wearily came to his feet. "He has succeeded there. My relationship with my daughter wasn't strong to start with, but now it's even shakier." He kneaded his temple. "I don't know about you, but I can't think about this anymore tonight. My brain feels like mush." He skirted the coffee table and stopped in front of her. "Tomorrow, no doubt, will be another long day. I'm determined to figure out who is after me. I don't like surprises, and lately my life has been one big surprise after another."

She smiled, clasping her hands into tight fists.

She wanted to touch him, soothe him and give him hope that everything would return to normalcy soon. She couldn't.

His eyes bored into hers as though searching deeply for something. "I understand now why you're so independent. I know I hired you to be Abbey's bodyguard, but you've gone beyond what I expected."

His warm appraisal jammed her throat with words she couldn't say to him. Besides Joshua, no one else knew what she'd gone through with Bryan. There was a part of her that was stunned she'd said anything to him; but there was a part that wasn't— because if she let herself she could fall for this man. Hard.

He cupped her face. "I hope you understand how important you are."

Those earlier tears threatened to surface again. She'd shed so many tears over her father and Bryan that she'd promised herself she wouldn't let anyone make her that vulnerable again. So why couldn't she stop herself from opening her heart to this man?

He lowered his mouth toward hers. He was so close that she felt the soft in-and-out of his breath, smelled the apple cider he'd drunk earlier. Her lips tingled right before he settled his on hers. He'd given her plenty of time to pull away. She couldn't have for the life of her. She wanted this kiss—had yearned for it since the last one.

He folded her against him, his arms caging her to him. The sense that she'd come home suffused throughout her as he deepened his possession of her mouth. In the back of her mind an alarm went off. She didn't care how dangerous this was. She welcomed the risk to feel special even if it was just for a moment.

When he broke off the kiss, he lay his forehead against hers, his breathing ragged. Her heart thumped so hard she wondered if he could feel it when he held her close.

He leaned back and stared into her eyes. "I know you can take care of yourself, but all I want to do is protect you, keep you safe."

His words sparked a memory of what Bryan had once told her when she rebelled against telling him where she'd been. *My job is to protect you. How can I if I don't know where you are?* It had been essential to Bryan to control her every move. That was his idea of protecting her.

The reminder sent the alarms clanging in her mind. She backed out of Slade's embrace.

ELEVEN

"That's okay. You're right." Elizabeth lifted her chin, squared her shoulders. "I'm capable of taking care of myself."

"I'm not denying that." Slade took a step toward her. She stiffened, and he went still. "But it doesn't change how I feel. Any man worth his salt wants to protect the people he cares about."

The implication of his statement robbed her of a reply. He cared about her. She cared about him. No, it couldn't be. Their lives were not compatible. She wanted something different from what he did. He was the kind of man who wanted a partner in marriage, and she had tried that—and lost herself to another. Yes, she'd dreamed of having a family at first with Bryan, but not at the expense of herself. She took another step back.

Across the expanse of a few feet, his gaze tangled with hers. "Don't let what your ex-husband did to you control everything you do. I had a healthy relationship with Catherine built on mutual respect and trust. You could have that, too."

Love wasn't an option for her. Look at what happened with her father and Bryan. Why set herself up for a third failure? She put more space between them. "I need to check the house. Make sure it's secured."

A shutter fell over his face. "Yes, you'd better do that. I need to get some sleep. Good night." With a nod, he strode out of the room, leaving behind a chill that burrowed its way into her heart.

She pivoted toward the Christmas tree, its lights, hooked up to a timer, still on. A beautifully hand-crafted ornament drew Elizabeth forward until she touched the soft lace on the dress of the little girl, a miniature of Abbey with long brown hair and brown eyes. Such love had gone into it. What would it be like to be a member of a family with that kind of love? Being here with Slade and Abbey made her wish her relationship was different with her father. Should she call him? Reach out one more time? Would it make a difference?

Her throat closed. Through a sheen of tears, she stared at the glittering lights that showcased such a memory-filled tree. Her childhood dreams stirred deeper inside her the longer she peered at the pine.

Then the lights blinked off, throwing the room into shadows.

She shook her childhood delusions from her mind and quickly headed out of the den before she actually started picturing herself in a home with a family.

After making her rounds to double-check that the house was secured and the fire in the den was dying down, Elizabeth trudged upstairs, tired but not sure how well she would sleep. As she passed Abbey's bedroom, she noticed a stream of light coming from under the teen's door. Changing directions, Elizabeth knocked on it.

Abbey opened her door a few inches.

"Can I come in?"

"To check my room? I can assure you no one is in it."

"No, to talk." Bosco, with his tail wagging, came up to be scratched. She bent down to greet him.

A question dimmed any defiance in Abbey's expression. She stepped to the side to allow Elizabeth inside. "Talk about what?"

"Tonight. The play. Whatever you want."

"What if I don't want to talk?"

"Then we won't, and I'll leave." Elizabeth straightened while Bosco trotted to Abbey's bed and hopped up on it.

"Why do you want to talk?"

Because I'm falling in love with your dad and I don't want to be alone with my thoughts. Because I know you're hurting and need someone to listen to you. "I don't, but I thought you might have questions about tonight."

"No, it's pretty simple to understand. Someone tried to hurt me. Now I have to stay locked up here at the ranch with no friends visiting." Running her hand along the dresser, Abbey strolled toward her bed as though she had not a care in the world.

"And you're okay with that?"

"Sure, what girl doesn't want to be stuck at home during the holidays when all her friends are going to the mall, to parties? And the best thing about my whole situation is that I have a maniac after me who wants to hurt me. I'd say just about any of my friends would die to change places with me." She snapped her fingers. "Oh, wait, they really might die if they changed places with me."

"Good. I'm glad you don't have any questions and are okay with everything." Elizabeth turned toward the door.

"Wait!"

Elizabeth peered over her shoulder at the teenage girl.

"Maybe I have one question." Abbey leaned into the bedpost, hugging it.

She swung back toward the girl.

"What if this maniac isn't found by Christmas? Will I be stuck here after the New Year?"

"You want me to tell you a piece of advice I

learned to follow when I worried about everything having to do with my future?"

Abbey frowned. "What?"

"If my worrying about the future and what might happen will change it, then I should. But if stewing over something I can't control won't change it, then I need to give my worries to God and let Him deal with them. Do you think you can change this situation by worrying?"

Abbey shook her head.

"Then I wouldn't waste my time. Use it instead to get to know your dad again. He's trapped here, too." Elizabeth moved a little closer to Abbey. "Tell you a secret. I don't think he's too thrilled about not being able to leave, either."

Abbey sank onto her bed, still clutching the bedpost, and rested her head against it. "This stinks."

"Yes, it does. But you can either be miserable or make the best of a bad situation. The choice is yours."

"Just like that, I can make it better?"

"I didn't say it would be easy, but your dad is doing the best he can to keep you safe. He feels the only way is here at the ranch where it is guarded while the police search for the person behind all this."

"But there are no leads."

"Some people on the list of suspects have been taken off. Others look promising and the police are concentrating on them. There's Paula Addison's boyfriend, Dwayne Olsen, who might be doing her bidding. Sam Howard moved back to the United States, not far from here, right before all this started. I don't like coincidences. Kevin Sharpe hasn't been found, and he has a reason to be upset with you and your dad. Jay Wilson is dead, but Joshua is trying to track down his family. He had two daughters and a son. So far only one daughter has been located. Lots of people are working on this, including your dad. He's been going through files and doing searches on the internet. He wants this over with as much as you do." There were a couple of others the police were delving into, but Abbey didn't need to know the names as much that something was being done to end her nightmare.

"It's not Kevin."

"Why do you say that?"

"Because he wouldn't know how to do what this person has been doing—an explosive device, shooting out a tire, cutting your brakes. Kevin was more like Dad, a computer geek. And I know for a fact, he hated the thought of killing even a bird. He couldn't understand why some boys in our class went hunting."

"But he's still missing and disappeared right before all this started."

"It's not him." Abbey loosened her tight grip on the bedpost.

"Have you told your dad why you don't think it's Kevin?"

"He wouldn't listen to me. I'm telling you."

"I'll pass it on, but your dad will listen to you."

"Sure, because he's got nothing better to do since he's stuck here, too."

Elizabeth rose. "Sarcasm isn't very becoming to you."

Abbey's eyes widened.

"Good night, Abbey. I'll see you in the morning. Remember, you control your attitude. Not the person after you." Elizabeth strolled toward the exit. When she glanced back at the teen as she shut the door, a thoughtful expression had replaced Abbey's defiant one.

Coming to work for Slade, Elizabeth hadn't realized she would be a referee between father and daughter. But she hoped she could help these two mend their differences. She hated to see their relationship end up estranged like hers with her dad.

Walking through the living room the following Thursday, Slade caught sight of a guard outside the large window that faced the front yard. He stopped and stared out, watching the man with a large German shepherd patrol the grounds, illuminated by the security lights that came on as he moved from one area to another. A second guard was thirty yards to the left. Abbey was right. This was just like a prison, with guards and everything. Except that he could hear Christmas music coming from the kitchen where Mary and Hilda were preparing dinner. It lightened his mood.

I wonder what Joshua and Elizabeth would say if I snuck out. Slade smiled for a few seconds at the picture of him making his great escape, then the gravity of the situation hit him square in the chest, sucking the breath from him. If he felt this way, no doubt Abbey experienced it even more, and yet she hadn't said much since the Saturday night of the play—five days before.

Five long days of nothing breaking on the case. The evidence the police found on the set's sabotage hadn't helped them garner any clues as to who was behind this. Neither had anything been found in the auditorium where the smoke bombs were remotely detonated. He even went through his video camera to see if he could find anything unusual, but the scenery that ended up falling blocked his view of backstage. And from Elizabeth's position, she couldn't see anyone behind the scenery either. Another dead end.

A noise behind him sent him flying around, his fists clenched as though readying himself to do battle.

"It's only me," Elizabeth said with a chuckle. "My stomach is rumbling. Whatever they are making smells wonderful."

"Roast beef with vegetables, homemade rolls and for dessert, a red velvet cake."

"Dessert? We don't usually indulge, thankfully, or I would have to exercise even more."

"Mary is trying to get us into the Christmas spirit. The cake was the centerpiece for the holiday open house that we won't have this year."

"It's usually a big deal?"

"We invite friends, employees at headquarters, people we want to thank. We also take donations to the Silver Chase Food Bank. Everyone brings a toy to contribute to the church toy drive for children who have one or both parents in prison. That part of Christmas I've always enjoyed. I can't say I was too much into the rest of the holidays. I thought of what it was like when my wife was alive. Maybe it's time to start some new traditions."

"That's not something I can help you with. I have no Christmas traditions. I never know where I'll be each year."

"Isn't that lonely?"

Elizabeth's eyebrows scrunched together. "I was always with people, standing back and watching their Christmas celebration or lack thereof, but yes, it is lonely."

"So we've both avoided the holidays for different reasons."

"Yeah, you had fond memories. I didn't."

"Our memories can be precious, but not when they stop us from moving forward."

"Or our memories can be ones best left totally in the past but still have a hold on us that we haven't been able to shake."

"We can always make new memories."

Her mouth tilted up in a smile that went straight to his heart. "To replace the old?"

He nodded. "Mary wants us to sing Christmas songs this evening after dinner. She says that's what she misses most this year."

"So that's why we're hearing them right now. Actually, for a good part of the past few days."

"Yep. She found a radio station that plays Christmas music 24/7 until the twenty-fifth."

"She wouldn't want to hear me sing. I can't carry a tune."

"To Mary, that doesn't matter."

"You've never talked about your own parents. Are they alive?"

He missed his parents and wished his mom were here to give him advice with Abbey. "No. My father died ten years ago and my mother a few years later. I think she died of a broken heart even though the official cause was a stroke. But at least both of them got to see and know Abbey."

Elizabeth ran her hand along the back of a wing chair. "I'm thinking of calling my father to wish him a merry Christmas."

"You are? What made you decide to do that?"

"You."

"Me? How?"

"Our discussions about moving on. Not letting the past dictate our future. I won't be able to until I can tell my father I forgive him. He might not think he needs to be forgiven, but I need to do it. I need to have some closure on my childhood." She moved away from him, prowling the living room as though restlessness had taken hold of her. "I don't know if I can do it. I even tried a few days ago and hung up before it rang."

Since he'd met her, she had inspired him to live for the present. He needed to make some changes or he would lose his daughter. Working all the time hadn't been the best answer to dealing with his grief. Certainly not for Abbey. "But you found the courage to make the attempt. You'll do it when it feels right."

"My goal is by Christmas. Life's too short to let this anger consume me."

"That a good—"

"Dad, Elizabeth!"

Abbey's urgent shout from the second floor landing propelled him across the living room and out into the foyer, Elizabeth next to him, her hand going to her gun. His daughter, her face drained of color, clutched the railing on the second floor.

"I got an email from…" Her voice grew raspier until she couldn't say anything.

With Elizabeth slightly ahead of him, Slade took the stairs two at a time.

Abbey turned toward them, one hand still gripping the banister so tight her knuckles were white. Lifting an arm that shook, she pointed toward her bedroom. "It's still on the computer. It's about you, Dad."

As Slade charged down the hallway, Elizabeth stayed with Abbey. He crossed his daughter's room and saw the email, titled From a Friend, on the screen. The address from one of the free online services didn't mean anything to him. Elizabeth came up behind him when he began reading the message, "I haven't forgotten you, Slade. I'm coming soon. A friend."

"Dad, it's from him, isn't it?"

He focused on the trembling in his daughter's voice, not the words on the screen. She needed him at the moment. Pivoting, he drew her against him. "Probably. But the good thing is that we might be able to track this email to its source."

Abbey bent back and looked up at him. "You can do that?"

"I should be able to."

"Why did he send it to me?"

"To terrify you. But he also thought the email would more likely get to you and you would read it—I've got too many filters up for it to get through to me."

"I thought it was from someone I met online."

"Honey, this really might be a good thing. Let me see what I can find out. Why don't you go downstairs and see if Gram wants any help with dinner? It should be ready soon."

"I can't help you?"

"One day I'll show you some of my tricks, but I can work faster when I don't have anyone watching over my shoulder."

Abbey grinned. "I'm gonna keep you to that promise when this is all over with."

He clasped her upper arms and looked straight into his daughter's face, which now had a little color. "We'll be spending a lot more time together. I have to admit, not as much as we have these past few days, but I'll be cutting back on work. Lately, my company has functioned fine without my presence all the time."

"You mean that?"

"Yep. You're the most important person to me." And that was why the person had sent the message to Abbey. Another taunt. This had to end soon, one way or another.

As Abbey left the room, Elizabeth stayed behind. "I'll let Joshua know what has happened. Once you get a location, the police can move on it."

"I know I'm getting my hopes up, but he's got to make a mistake. I'm hoping this is it."

Slade greeted the sheriff in the foyer late the next afternoon. "Thanks for coming out here. Let's go into my office."

"Where is everyone?" Sheriff McCain followed Slade.

"In the kitchen making snacks for tonight."

"Tonight?"

"Elizabeth had thought 'the girls' should have a movie night with snacks and everything."

"Girls?"

"Mary, Hilda, Cindy, Abbey and Elizabeth. I wasn't invited, so I dubbed it the girls' night in."

"Probably a good thing you weren't invited. You should see some of the sappy movies my wife drags me to."

In his office, Slade gestured toward two chairs. "So what have you all been able to track down?"

"We went through the videotapes of the internet café where the email you received was sent. Using the time on the email, we were able to narrow the suspects down to three people. Before we interview them, I wanted to show you their pictures to see if you know one of them." The sheriff slid three photos out of a manila envelope and passed them to Slade.

He flipped through them. Two were young men,

at the most only a few years older than Abbey. The last one was a balding man of about forty. "I don't know them. What are their names?"

"On the backs of the photos."

Slade examined each picture and then turned them over to see what the names were. "Still don't mean anything to me. Are you sure these were the only people in the café at that time?"

"Yes, the owner said it had been a slow night. A couple of ladies came in, got some coffee and left. That was all."

"I think we should show these to Abbey to see if she knows one of them."

"Good suggestion."

Slade pushed to his feet and headed toward where Abbey, Elizabeth, Cindy, Mary and Hilda were.

"I saw Joshua when I arrived," the sheriff said as they came to the entrance into the kitchen.

"Yeah, he's checking the grounds. He likes to periodically make sure the cameras are working and there are no breaches in the perimeter."

"What are they making? It smells delicious."

"Smells like cookies. Mary said something about Christmas ones they could decorate."

"And she got your sixteen-year-old to go along with it?"

Slade chuckled. "Yes, which shows you the depth of my daughter's boredom. Maybe with Elizabeth and Cindy here tonight she won't feel totally surrounded by us old fogies."

Abbey, with flour on her green sweater, peered toward him and the sheriff when they entered the room. Butter knife in hand, Elizabeth finished icing a snowman cookie and put it on the waxed paper for Abbey to decorate. The scene before Slade, the air laced with the aroma of sugar cookies and hot apple cider on the stove, made him wish the lawman was only at the ranch for a social visit.

"What's up, Dad?"

"Sheriff McCain has some photos to show you. Where's Hilda?"

Mary dried her hands on a towel. "She wasn't feeling very well and went to her room to lie down. She's coming down with a cold."

With Bosco planted at her feet, Abbey rose and joined Slade. "Let me see. Is this the person who sent me the email?"

Sheriff McCain gave her the envelope, and she went through the pictures. Tiny lines wrinkled her forehead.

"Do you know one of them?" Slade spied the photo his daughter lingered over—the middle-aged man.

"I've seen him somewhere." Abbey held up the picture for her grandmother to see. "Gram, doesn't he go to our church?"

Mary retrieved her reading glasses from the chain

around her neck and studied the photo of the balding man. "Yes, I think he does. He doesn't come regularly, but I remember him being at the late service a month ago, right before Thanksgiving."

Hope flared in Slade. This was the break they needed. "Do you all recognize either of the young men?"

"Nope," Abbey immediately said, while Mary and Cindy examined each picture for a long moment.

"I don't, either," his mother-in-law finally said.

"This one looks familiar, but I can't place where I've seen him." Cindy pointed to the young man named Matt Alton. "Maybe I saw him with Brody. He looks about the same age."

"Thanks, ladies. This is a big help," the sheriff said, taking the pictures back from Cindy.

"I'll walk you out." In the foyer Slade opened the front door. "Let me know what you find out after you interview them. It's about time he made a mistake."

"Will do." Sheriff McCain rubbed the back of his neck. "But just because the man goes to the same church doesn't mean anything really. There are only so many churches in the area."

"But at least it's something. According to the Dallas police, the smoke bomb didn't lead anywhere. Nothing has panned out there yet."

"I just didn't want you to get your hopes up too much. I'll call you later."

Slade closed the door and leaned back against it, his eyes sliding shut. *Lord, is this the beginning of the end of this ordeal? Please, I hope so.*

"What did the sheriff say?" Elizabeth's soft voice curled around him as if it were a blanket warming him in the cold.

He lifted his eyelids and saw her beautiful features not three feet away. He wanted to kiss her again, but he wasn't going to until this was over. He needed to stay focused on the person after him and Abbey. And yet the sight of her full lips mocked that decision.

"He'll call me after he's interviewed the guys. Maybe I'll crash your 'girls only' party tonight."

"Feeling left out?"

"Yeah, but if Abbey is happy—and safe—that's all I care about." Slade shoved away from the front door.

"I'm glad to see you two have been getting along lately. She hasn't whined nearly as much as she did the week before."

"I think Brody has something to do with that," Slade said. "His tutoring sessions with Abbey have been extra long. I know math isn't her forte, but really, three hours Monday and Wednesday nights."

"What I want to know is what happened to Tuesday and Thursday?"

"Basketball games. He's on the squad."

"Look on the bright side. She didn't bug you about going to the games."

"But how long can I keep this up? Abbey is like her mother. Very social."

Elizabeth laid her hand on his arm. "As long as necessary. Something will give. I don't see this person waiting too much longer."

The touch of her fingers momentarily centered his attention on Elizabeth, her expression full of compassion that drew him to her. "And that's what I'm worried about the most," Slade finally said.

The screen in the theater room went dark as the movie ended. Why had she watched *It's a Wonderful Life?* The last time she had, she'd cried and Bryan had made fun of her. She'd thought she'd stamped out all softness in the years since her marriage broke up. But there was something about being at the ranch with Slade's family at Christmas that was making her emotional. Bryan had always said her tears were a sign of weakness. While she told herself she didn't really believe him, deep down there was a part that did.

Then she remembered the call she'd finally placed to her father before dinner hours ago. He hadn't been home, but she'd left him a message that she wanted to talk to him. Relief that she'd finally made the call mingled with dread that her father would call back when she wasn't mentally prepared to talk to him.

The overhead lighting flicked on, and Elizabeth twisted around in the lounge chair before the big screen. Slade stood inside the entrance.

"I didn't know anyone was in here. I thought you all went upstairs a while ago."

"Cindy left. Abbey went to bed. I decided to come back here and watch another movie." Elizabeth averted her head and wiped the remnants of her tears away.

Slade moved in front of her. "Have you been crying? What's wrong?" He sank into the chair next to hers.

Flitting her hand in the air between them, she murmured, "Nothing."

"Did your dad return your call?"

"No." She could tell he wouldn't give up until she told him why she'd been crying. "We watched some Christmas movies, and after escorting Abbey to her bedroom, I came back to see *It's a Wonderful Life*. I saw it in your movie collection and remembered as a child watching it every Christmas. It always made me cry."

"But the message is hopeful."

"I know. I guess I always hoped someday my father would declare his love and how important I am in his life."

"It's his—" The ringing of Slade's cell interrupted

the rest of his sentence. He answered his phone and listened intently before saying, "A woman? That changes everything. I'll tell Joshua and Elizabeth. I'll have to rethink a few things."

Elizabeth pushed her sad thoughts from her mind and sat up straight. "What is it?" she asked when Slade hung up.

"That was the sheriff. They focused on the man from the church but couldn't tie him to anything. He had an alibi for Saturday night, and when your brakes were cut, he was out of town on business. Matt Alton also had an alibi for Saturday night. He'd been on a hunting trip with his dad and some friends. But the third interview panned out. Faced with the sheriff and deputy in his house, Ben James admitted to being paid to send that email. He was instructed to send it from the public library, but he forgot it closed at five on Thursdays so he used the internet café to send the message."

"Who paid him?"

"He doesn't know who she is, but he's positive it was a woman. Curious who would pay him a hundred dollars to send an email, he staked out the drop-off site for the person who contacted him by phone. He said the voice over the phone could have been either a man or woman."

"Was it mechanical sounding like the call to you?"

"No, just disguised. But it was definitely a woman

who left the money, although he didn't see her face. It was covered by a hoodie."

"How convenient. How did this Ben know it was a woman?"

"The sheriff said he described the body as petite, slight."

"Now the question is, was the woman the actual person or sent by the person?"

Slade slipped his cell back in his pocket. "I don't know. But if it's a woman, who could that be? Paula Addison is in prison and everyone else on that list is male."

"Maybe we're looking at it wrong. For instance, Jay Wilson committed suicide, and we have only been able to find one of his children—the youngest daughter—but not his son or other daughter. And what if the person Ben saw was a young teenage boy like Kevin Sharpe? Kevin isn't tall or heavily built. From a distance he might look like a female." But Elizabeth remembered Abbey's conviction that it wasn't Kevin, and she'd had some good points.

"All I know is that I'm glad you and Joshua are here. I feel like I have a chance against this phantom person, whether female or male." He took Elizabeth's hand, his touch compelling her to look into his eyes.

"That's our job. To make your life safer and hopefully easier." Her words rushed together because the expression in his gray depths unnerved her.

"I know a lot has happened in a short time, but having you here has made it bearable, not just for me but for Abbey, too. She responds to you and for that, I'm thankful." He tugged her closer, only the arms of the two chairs between them. Reaching out, he framed her face with his hands. "I'm not sure I have words to tell you how grateful I am."

"I'm only doing my job." But her fast pulse rate belied that declaration. There was much more between her and Slade than an assignment, which was what frightened her. Her heart had been wounded twice. She didn't want to go through it again, and she and Slade were from two different worlds.

He leaned over the arms of the chairs and brushed his mouth over hers. "I never thought I would take off my wedding ring. I didn't think I ever would find someone else who I could love. I thought I'd had my one love and it wasn't possible to have another, but this feeling I have for you isn't going away. It grows each day I'm with you. I'm in love with you and want to continue seeing you even after your job is over. You don't have to say anything now, but think about it."

She could face down a person with a gun, but right now with Slade, his declaration sent fear through her. He was in love with her, and all she could think about was how messed up her first marriage had been, even if her feelings for Slade were strong. Possibly love. And there was her job. One that had given her a sense of who she was.

The sound of Bosco's yap and the padding of his paws across the wooden floor in the theater room took Elizabeth by surprise. She seized on the distraction to avoid answering Slade. "What are you doing down here? Is Abbey on the phone again and ignoring you?" Her terrier mix leaped into her lap and gave another yelp.

"More likely that's it. A male can only take so much." Slade scratched her dog behind his ears. "Us males have to stick together, don't we?"

Bosco answered him with a bark.

A vague feeling nagged at her. As if she was missing something. "You should tell Joshua about what the sheriff said. Maybe if we sleep on it, we can meet tomorrow morning and go through the list of suspects again with the idea it might be a woman—or a slightly built man. Another question we need to consider is how the person knew to contact Ben James."

"I'll call the sheriff back and have him look into that and then let Joshua know what's going on."

Bosco licked Elizabeth's face. "Now you want my lovin'. The second you arrived here you abandoned me for Abbey." She rubbed her face against her pet.

The vague feeling evolved into a sense that something wasn't right. She got to her feet, putting Bosco on the floor, then started for the hallway. "Why is Bosco out of the room? He's rarely been away from Abbey since he came here. Even if she's on the phone, how did he get out?"

"Abbey let him out?"

"Maybe, but he usually stays in the hall outside her door, whining to get back in. It never hurts to check." Elizabeth checked the downstairs security system and exhaled deeply when she noticed it was still on.

Slade trailed her steps all the way up the stairs and down the long corridor to Abbey's room. He rapped on the door. No answer.

Apprehension leaked into his expression while Elizabeth thrust open the door.

Bosco darted into the room and began yelping at the bathroom door.

Elizabeth followed. The sound of the shower running drifted to her. A frisson of relief eased some of her tension.

But when Bosco continued to bark, Elizabeth's internal alarm system went off. She marched to the bathroom door and knocked. After a minute she tried the knob. It was locked. "Abbey, open up," she shouted to be heard over the shower.

After a moment of waiting, Slade tugged Elizabeth out of the way and raised his leg, kicking in the bathroom door. It slammed against the wall. He rushed in with Elizabeth right behind him. The empty room taunted her. Then her attention fell on the open window with a ladder—one usually stored in the bathroom cabinet in case of a fire—hooked to the ledge.

TWELVE

"The alarm should have gone off if the window was opened." Slade walked to where the ladder was and leaned out of the window.

"Not if she turned off the security system upstairs and left the one on downstairs. The one we check more often." Elizabeth kept her voice calm while inside every muscle tensed.

"Why?"

"To see Brody, maybe. Let's check her room and the security system."

"I'll check the alarm." Slade strode into the hallway.

Elizabeth circled the room, searching for anything out of the ordinary. At Abbey's desk she found a note, handwritten, partially under the keyboard.

When Slade reentered, a muscle in his cheek jerked. "It's off."

Waving the note, Elizabeth said, "She went to meet Brody. She left this, so if for some reason we came in here, we wouldn't panic. She just wanted to spend some time alone with him. She was tired of always being watched."

"Why the ladder? Why not just go out the front door?"

"Because the camera would catch her leaving. She didn't want anyone to know. She was probably afraid the security company would alert you since it's late."

"I hope she has her phone with her, because I'm going to give her a piece of my mind." He took out his cell and punched in a number. When he disconnected a moment later, a frown marred his expression. "It went to voice mail."

"Something feels wrong." Elizabeth strode from the room and toward the staircase. As she descended the steps, she peered at Slade. His expression mirrored his obvious exasperation at his daughter, but it also held fear. What if Brody had set Abbey up?

"Where do you think she went?" His jaw clamped down on the last word.

"The perimeter has cameras along it. So do the entrances to this house and the barn. I'm going to the bunkhouse and barn. You call Jake and see if he knows anything, and have Joshua check the video feed of the cameras around the ranch and make sure all of them are working." There was a room where several computers were set up for him to do this on-site even though they were monitored off-site.

"Also notify the guards at the gates. See if anyone came or left."

Slade fished in his pocket for his cell.

After switching off the alarm, Elizabeth went to the front door. "We need to get moving on this."

Slade paused in his trek toward the den. "You're scaring me."

"You should be scared. I don't have a good feeling about this."

Elizabeth didn't wait for Slade to reply. She quickly left and headed for the bunkhouse first. A clock materialized in her mind, ticking off the seconds that Abbey was missing. Waving to one of the security guards, she slipped through the gate and strode down the paved road to the barn. She saw the lights on in the bunkhouse and the darkened hull of the barn, only a soft, muted glow coming from its interior.

Her knock at the bunkhouse door was answered by Hank. "Howdy, miss. What's up?"

"Is Brody here?"

"Nope. He left a while back, all gussied up."

"Do you know where he was going?"

"Nah, that one is closemouthed. Can't get much out of him."

"Who else is here?" Elizabeth peered around Hank.

"Just Gus. The other two went into town." He

winked at her. "It's Friday night. They always go
to the local bar. Something wrong?"

"Abbey's gone. She's supposed to be with
Brody."

Hank shifted around and called out, "Gus, come
here." When the other cowhand appeared, he continued. "Did Brody tell you what he was doing
tonight?"

Gus dragged his hand through his short-cropped
hair. "Naw. But he doused himself in aftershave.
Stunk the bathroom up."

"Thanks. If you see him or Abbey, give the house
a call." She turned away.

"Do you need our help?"

Eagerness mixed with concern greeted her glance
back at the pair. "If one of you can check out the
barn and the other stay here in case Brody comes
back, that would be great." She doubted they were
meeting in the barn because of the cameras on the
exterior doors, but it didn't hurt to check.

On the short hike back to the main house to
find out what Joshua and Slade had discovered,
she checked to see if Brody's old beat-up truck was
parked in its usual place. It was, which meant that
Abbey was probably still somewhere on the ranch.
At least she hoped so. She tried to figure out where
Abbey would have gone. The ranch was huge, and
only the perimeter was lined with cameras.

Back in the main house she walked directly to the

room where the computers were. Joshua was at the bank of monitors, running through the feed. With the stance of a warrior, Slade stood behind him.

"Anything?"

"Nothing on the perimeter cameras. No one has entered or left the ranch in the past hour." Joshua typed in a command and another screen popped up. "The people off-site didn't notice anything unusual."

"Then she's still here. That does narrow it down slightly." Elizabeth looked at Slade. "Have you tried her again on her cell?"

"Five minutes ago. It still goes to voice mail."

"Are you tracking her GPS in her cell?" she asked when she saw what Joshua pulled up.

"Yeah. I've got a location. It's by the bunk-house."

"I was just there. I didn't see anything."

"It's behind the bunkhouse, about ten yards or so." Joshua pointed to the computer.

"What's there?" Elizabeth again replayed her walk back to the house, but she hadn't seen anything unusual.

"A pasture. A grove of trees isn't too far from the bunkhouse. Do you think they met there?" Slade kneaded his thumb into his palm.

Joshua scooted back his chair. "Only one way to find out. Elizabeth and I will search the area."

"I'm coming, too."

Joshua blocked the doorway. "Nope. You're paying me to protect you, and that's what I aim to do. If Abbey has been taken, we don't know what this person, male or female, is going to do. You need to stay in here with the alarm on. Nothing may be wrong. We still need someone to be with Mary and Hilda. I'll post the guards at the doors to the house until we get back. I'll call when we know something."

"I need to be out there looking for Abbey."

Joshua shook his head. "We don't know if she's really missing. What if she's perfectly fine, but something happens to you because you rush out and do something stupid?"

For a long moment Slade's gaze bore into Joshua. Anger flowed off Slade in waves, but finally he nodded.

After Joshua grabbed a couple of flashlights and gave instructions to the security guards outside, Elizabeth left the house with her uncle and hurried toward the bunkhouse. Switching on the light, she searched the terrain for any sign of Abbey or Brody. She and her uncle climbed over the fence right behind the bunkhouse and went farther out into the pasture toward the grove Slade described.

As Elizabeth neared the small cluster of trees, she called Abbey's cell, hoping it would ring nearby. Only silence greeted her. The almost-full moon cast eerie shadows off the bare branches, which swayed in the cool breeze. A shiver snaked up Elizabeth's spine as though evil itself touched her.

To the left of her she spied a mound on the ground near the base of a large oak that had retained its dead leaves. "Joshua, I've found something," she called as she closed the distance between her and the lump, "or, rather, someone."

Slade gathered Mary and Hilda in the den, so he could keep an eye on them as he waited to hear back from Joshua and Elizabeth. He paced from one end of the room to the other while Mary and Hilda prayed on the couch.

This feeling of waiting brought back all the emotions that had inundated him when Catherine had died and he'd had to stand by and do nothing. He couldn't save her. Even his prayers, he'd felt, had gone unanswered.

God, are You turning Your back on me again? Don't let Abbey be harmed. Bring her home safely. Whatever You want, I'll give You.

When his cell rang in his hand, he flinched. *Please be good news.*

As he answered the call, he noticed the number was blocked, which sent his heartbeat racing. "Slade here."

"Ah, it's been a while since we talked," the person said in a disguised voice as though trying to mask his—or her—gender.

He stepped away so Hilda and Mary wouldn't be able to hear him. "What have you done with Abbey?"

"She's safe if you follow my directions. Your daughter's life will depend on you doing exactly as I say. First, get somewhere alone. Go into your office."

He strode out of the room and made his way to his office. "I'm alone now."

"I'll trade you for your daughter. Do you love her enough to do that?" The person didn't wait for an answer. "You can't tell anyone where you're going. If anyone follows you, I'll know and kill Abbey. I have ways of listening."

Were more bugs somehow planted in the past few days, by someone who'd been in his house recently? A supposed friend?

"When you go to the old cabin at the back of the ranch, I'll call that woman you care so much about and tell her where I hid Abbey."

"Please don't hurt my daughter. I'll trade myself for her. I'll do anything you say."

"Good. Because it's you I want, not Abbey."

"How will I know my daughter is safe?"

A laugh, definitely feminine, sounded. "You just got to trust me. Leave your cell at your house. If I discover it on you, your daughter is dead. You've got fifteen minutes to get to the cabin without anyone else. If you are a minute late, I'll detonate the bomb attached to Abbey."

"A bomb on Abbey? I can't make the cabin in fifteen minutes." He could only ride a horse part of the way. The rest of the terrain was too risky in the dark.

"If you leave *right* now, yes, you can."

Please don't be Abbey. Please be alive.

She knelt by the body and shone the flashlight at the face. Brody. Feeling for a pulse at the side of his neck, she nearly collapsed with relief when she discovered a steady beat beneath her fingertips. Joshua joined her, his light revealing the young man's bound hands and feet while Elizabeth found the matted blood on his head. Then they both swung their flashlights in a wide arc around Brody.

"Abbey's gone." Elizabeth picked up the teen's cell phone next to Brody. It vibrated in her palm. Clutching it, she answered it. "Yes."

"You can find Abbey at the lake tied to a tree," a voice that could be either male or female said.

"Who—" The call disconnected.

Joshua rolled Brody onto this back and placed his own call to 911, then asked, "Who was that?"

"The person who took Abbey. He, she, I couldn't tell, told me I could find her tied to a tree by the lake."

Joshua rose. "Why? Another game?"

"I have a bad feeling about this. Have since it started tonight."

"We need more manpower to search the lake. There are a lot of trees out there."

"I'm going to the lake to start the search while you go get more help. Abbey is my responsibility," she added when Joshua started to protest, "and I *will* find her."

A brisk wind came off the lake as Elizabeth reached the shore with only a flashlight and moonlight to illumine her path. Trekking over the uneven ground, she shone her light on the tree line. A sense of urgency swamped her. The noise of the water lapping against the rocky beach couldn't mask the thundering of her heartbeat in her ears.

Her cell ringing cut through the sound of a hoot owl in a pine up ahead. Elizabeth answered on the second ring. "Yes."

"Slade is gone. He got a call and left the house."

The tight thread in her uncle's voice heightened her fear that this wouldn't end well. "Why?"

"Mary is sure the call came from the person behind all this. Worse, I can't track him with his cell—I found it on the hall table. Mary listened to Slade talking in his office, and she heard something about a cabin. She says there's one on the ranch in the northwest pasture on the back property line."

"I just reached the lake and am starting my search."

"The lake is between the cabin and the main house. The ambulance should be here any minute and the sheriff's ETA is five minutes. Once everyone has arrived, I'll head to the lake. Mary thinks Slade is trading himself for his daughter. We need to find Abbey and make sure she is safe, then go looking for Slade. I believe there's a bomb on Abbey, so be careful. I'm leaving right now. The sheriff has called in the bomb squad, but we might not have the time. Once you find her, give me your location and I'll disarm it."

She thanked God that her uncle had been on the bomb squad for years before rising to the level of captain in the Dallas police department. "You'll see my light. I'm on the east side making my way north."

The dark shape of the old cabin loomed before Slade as he ran the last part of his trip. He checked his watch and noted one minute until his time was up. Sweat drenched him. His heart pounded with each step he took.

Lord, anything You want. Just save my daughter. Take me if You must.

A hundred yards to go.

Slade counted down the time in his mind and pressed forward, increasing his speed as much as possible in the darkness with only a flashlight to show him the path. Leaping over a fallen trunk, he headed down a small incline, then up the other side of the ditch. Slipping in the grass, he stumbled forward, caught himself before falling and charged forward.

Twenty yards.

His breath hissed from him in short bursts. He reached the cabin with ten seconds to spare. Shining the light on the entrance, he saw the door wide open. He made his way to it and entered the cabin.

He stood in the middle of the large, almost bare room layered with dust and cobwebs and swung around in a full circle, noting the empty table and two chairs, a cupboard with a missing door, a dirty rug over part of the floor. "I'm here. Show yourself. You've got what you want. Me."

Silence.

He hadn't heard a bomb go off, so he prayed that meant Abbey was still alive. He backed away from the entrance, moving deeper into the shadows.

"Are you too scared to show yourself? Or, are you going to continue to hide behind all these little games you've played?"

"On the contrary, I'm right here, and relishing every minute of this." Cindy stood in the doorway to the cabin with a gun in one hand and a flashlight in the other. "I've been thinking about this moment ever since my father, Jay Wilson, killed himself. He couldn't face going to prison if he was convicted. His life became a living nightmare. I decided to make yours like that so you'd know how it feels to have things totally out of your control."

He wanted to laugh at that statement. He'd learned long ago his life wasn't in his control. And now he had to place it in the Lord's hands because he didn't know how he would get out of this alive.

Cindy gestured with her gun to her right. "Pick that detonator up."

Slade did, his hand shaking as he held it.

"If you set off the detonator, your daughter dies but you live. I'll walk away and never bother you again. You control your daughter's destiny. So what will you do?"

The sounds of voices back along the shoreline, following her path, filtered to Elizabeth. She waved her flashlight in the air to show them where she was, then returned to searching for Abbey. Each second could be the child's last one, and she was determined to find her before she was harmed.

Up ahead, about ten yards away, she saw something that looked like a person sitting against a large pine. Running, praying it was Abbey, Elizabeth covered the short distance in seconds. Her light illuminated the frightened, wide-eyed expression on Abbey's face. A gag stuffed in her mouth, a rope circling the teen and tree and a bomb strapped to the girl's chest sent terror through Elizabeth. She allowed herself a moment of that emotion before she shut it down. She had to remain calm and keep Abbey calm.

Kneeling in front of the girl, Elizabeth loosened the cloth around Abbey, who then spat out the rag in her mouth. "Don't move. I don't know what triggers this bomb. Joshua will be here in a minute. He knows all about these things. Understand?"

Tears trickling from her eyes, Abbey said, "Yes."

Her raw, shaky voice worried Elizabeth. "Remember, stay calm. Don't move. I won't leave you."

"Where's Daddy?"

Cindy pointed the gun toward her left. "Pick up that detonator, too."

Slade saw it in the glow of his light on the floor a few feet from him. He bent over and grasped it. Ice seemed to replace the blood in his veins.

"You have a choice." She backed away from the doorway. "You can either detonate the one that you just picked up and blow yourself up, or you can detonate the other and blow up your daughter. I'll give you two minutes to make the decision, and don't think about leaving the cabin. I've nailed shut the windows. This door is the only way out, and I'll be covering it." Clicking off her flashlight, she slid on night-vision goggles and took another step away. "I have a second remote for your bomb, and I'll make the choice for you if you don't choose in two minutes. You control your destiny one last time."

The sound of the door slamming jolted Slade. He stared at it, his mind totally blank for a precious moment. Then he began to quake as he looked down at the devices in his hands. Left, he was dead. Right, Abbey was. If he could believe Cindy.

Lord, there's no choice.

Joshua worked to defuse the bomb strapped to Abbey. It had been a while since he'd done this, but Elizabeth knew her uncle kept up all the skills he'd acquired over the years.

"Elizabeth, I've got this covered. I'm almost done. You need to take some of the men and head to the cabin. Abbey will be fine, and I'll be right behind you as soon as I finish up here."

"Cabin?" Abbey mumbled.

"Your dad is there." Joshua took his wire cutters out of his pocket while a guard trained a heavy-duty flashlight on the bomb.

"Why?"

Joshua glanced back at Elizabeth, his mouth pinched into a frown.

She stooped down next to her uncle. "I believe you need to know the truth, but remember you have to stay calm. Your dad traded himself for you."

"No, he can't. She'll kill him. She wants him dead."

"She? Who?"

"Jake's wife, Cindy. She's crazy. She laughed about how no one knew she could shoot so well or build explosives. Her dad taught her. Kept going on about how Dad killed her father, so she was gonna even the score."

Elizabeth rose. "I'll do everything I can to make sure that doesn't happen."

Jake stepped forward. "Cindy is behind this?"

Abbey stared up at him, fear mingling with anger. "Yes. She used you. Even Brody. She laughed about that, too."

Elizabeth motioned to three guards. "Let's go."

"I want to come." Jake moved into her path.

"I think you should stay here."

"No. I know the fastest way to the cabin. Time is of the essence."

The fury on the man's face convinced Elizabeth she had to take the risk and let him come. "Fine." But she would keep a sharp eye on him.

With the three security personnel and Jake, Elizabeth left her uncle and the one guard working on defusing the bomb and headed northwest from the lake.

Jake directed them to the west. "The terrain is easier this way."

Did she make a mistake trusting the man?

Five minutes later Jake ran up an incline. "It's not far." At the top he pointed toward a dark area with lots of trees.

As Elizabeth hurried down the small rise, an explosion blasted the night.

THIRTEEN

The loud boom rocked Elizabeth as a glow lit the night. Smoke billowed from the tops of the trees—a gray cloud in the midst of the dark. She was too late. She went to her knees. For a few seconds she allowed despair to ravage her.

Slade!

His name screamed through her mind as she scrambled to her feet and rushed into the grove surrounding the cabin. Through the trees, she saw the mound of rubble from the blast.

As she approached, she scanned the area. Where was Cindy? The thought that she was out here some-where constricted Elizabeth's stomach into a knot. She slowed her step and motioned to the others to spread out and surround the cabin.

Glock in hand, Elizabeth proceeded forward, trying not to think of what she would find. Behind her, she heard more people coming over the last incline. The cavalry. Too late.

At close range, that realization grew even firmer

in her mind when she spied the extent of the damage in the clearing. Smoke from the blast hung in the air. There was no fire that she could see in the dim light, but the destruction was still unmistakable.

Surveying what she could see of the remains reinforced in her mind that Slade couldn't have survived the explosion. Her heart broke. Earlier he'd told her he was in love with her, and she couldn't tell him she was falling in love with him. She'd been too scared to say the words. Now she would never be able to. Tears of fury and overwhelming sadness inundated her, and yet she had no time to cry—not with all that needed to be done.

Joshua disengaged from the sheriff and two of his deputies and came up to her side, settling his hand on her shoulder. "Are you all right?"

No, never again. She started to nod her head but couldn't. Instead she murmured, "No. Why did this happen?"

"I don't know why. We may not know what happened here until morning."

An eternity to leave Slade buried among the debris while Cindy got away. "We've got to find Cindy."

"The sheriff's got that covered with his deputies. At least the bomb didn't set off a fire. With these trees surrounding the cabin we would have had a problem."

"I don't see much silver lining in this situation."

The pressure in her chest trapped each breath in her lungs. She had to force herself to breathe, but it did little to relieve the constriction. "Where's Abbey?"

"I had the guard take her back to the house. She doesn't need to see this."

No one did. She had to do something, or she would fall apart. "I'm gonna look…" Her throat closed around the last word in the sentence.

She finally holstered her Glock and started toward what was left of the cabin.

"You should stay back," one of the security guards said. "The sheriff has the fire department on its way."

Elizabeth ignored the man. She didn't care. She needed to find Slade. See with her own eyes that he was dead.

Abbey screamed at the top of the incline when she crested the mound and looked down on the scene below. A guard, probably the one who was supposed to escort her back to the main house, came up beside the teen and took her arm. She jerked free and raced down to the cabin, not stopping until she saw Elizabeth.

Abbey hugged Elizabeth and sobbed. "He can't be dead. He can't be."

For a few seconds her arms hung loosely at her sides, numb with grief. *This is why I don't want to love someone. It hurts too much.* But slowly the sounds of Abbey's crying pulled her back to the present, a present where Slade's daughter needed comfort.

"I'm so sorry, Abbey." She wound her arms around the girl and held her tightly, trying to infuse what solace she could when she had so little.

Suddenly Abbey leaned back, her face wet with tears. "Maybe he hid in the storm cellar."

For just a second, hope flickered within her. "Storm cellar? Where?"

"Under the cabin." Abbey whirled around and pointed toward the northeast corner of the place. "We discovered it once when we were exploring the ranch. When my mom was alive. It's kinda creepy, but Dad said it was built to protect the people who lived here from tornadoes. There's a way in from the cabin and from the outside on the east side."

Elizabeth suppressed her excitement that Slade might have survived. But she grabbed Abbey's hand and tugged her forward. "Show me."

Abbey hurried toward the east side of what was left of the cabin. "There." Pieces of blown-up wood lay haphazardly over the area where the girl pointed.

"I need people over here to help me," Elizabeth shouted and began tossing the debris away from the spot.

Sheriff McCain, Joshua, Jake and a couple of the guards came to help.

"One of my deputies notified me that he picked up Cindy. He's taken her into custody."

Elizabeth peered at Jake, and even in the dim light from the various flashlights she could see the anger that tensed his face. She knew the look of betrayal and the pain he would go through because of Cindy. But she couldn't worry about that just now. Finding Slade was all that mattered.

Minutes later the last piece of wood was flung away from the storm cellar's opening. Elizabeth reached out a trembling hand and pulled on the latch. *Please let him be alive, Lord.*

Taking her flashlight, she went first down the ladder. The eerie quiet wrapped about her as though it were a shroud. What if he hadn't remembered the cellar? What if…

Her sweeping light as she moved forward in the narrow tunnel fell upon a mound of dirt and debris that collapsed from one wall and part of the ceiling of a small room. Trapped beneath it lay Slade, eyes closed, part of his body still visible.

She rushed forward as Joshua and the sheriff came down into the shelter. Kneeling as close to Slade as possible, she placed her fingers at the side of his neck. The beating of his pulse was an answer to her prayer. *Thank You, Lord.*

"He's alive. Let's get him out of here." Elizabeth tore at the debris that held him captive.

In Slade's hospital room hours later, Elizabeth stood back, leaning against the wall while Abbey hugged her father, tears streaming down her face.

"I'm so sorry I left my room to meet Brody. I didn't think anything like this would happen." She gulped in a deep breath. "I never imagined Cindy…" The rest of her sentence faded into the silence as the teen swiped the wet tracks from her cheeks and stepped back.

"Honey, I thought our place was safe. Although you and I will talk about the fact that you sneaked out of the house to meet a boy, I'm just glad it's over."

With a few cuts and bruises on his face and one nasty bump on his head, he looked exhausted but wonderfully alive to Elizabeth. The doctors had insisted he stay the rest of the night for observation before they let him go home tomorrow—she glanced at her watch—correction, later this morning.

"Dad, I've never been so scared in my life. I—" Abbey snapped her mouth closed, tears slipping from her eyes again.

Slade took her hand. "Me, too. All I wanted was to make sure you were all right."

"You—" Abbey paused "—traded yourself for

me—I love you, Dad." She threw her arms around him again and kissed him on the cheek.

"I love you, hon. No matter what."

Mary came forward. "I don't know about you, Abbey, but I'm ready to go home and get some sleep. Besides, your dad needs to rest because now that everything is back to normal, I intend to have the Christmas open house after all."

Slade groaned, but a grin plastered his face.

"We'll be back to pick you up." Abbey gave her father another kiss, then started for the door. She stopped in front of Elizabeth and said, "Thank you for everything you did for me. I'm alive because of you." Abbey embraced Elizabeth, then left the room.

Elizabeth swung her attention to Slade, knowing he was looking at her. She felt the caress of his gaze deep in the marrow of her bones. She shoved herself from the wall and covered the space between them. "I'd better be going, too."

He grasped her hand before she turned away. "Don't. Earlier, before your dog—who's getting a big steak, by the way—interrupted us, I told you I love you. When you didn't reply to that, I let it go for the time being. But after what nearly happened tonight, I'm not letting another minute go by without talking to you about how I feel and seeing where we stand. Life's too short. I found that out tonight when I was faced with dying."

And she'd faced his death tonight, too. She never wanted to go through that again, especially when she hadn't told him how she felt earlier. "I agree." Cupping her other hand over his, she moved as close to him as possible. "I don't know if I would have said anything earlier, because for the longest time I've been afraid of loving another person after my dad and Bryan. The risk just seemed too much. Then I almost lost you tonight, and I knew it would be far worse to not grab hold of the gift you'd given me for fear of what might or might not happen. Even if my father never calls, I tried and I've forgiven him. I need to move on."

He started to say something. She placed her finger over his lips. "With you. I love you, Slade Caulder. You're nothing like Bryan, but then I'm not like I was when I married him. I know how important it is to stand up for myself, to be me, not some vision someone else has of me. Can you accept me as I am?"

His eyes lit with a silver fire. "That's the only way I'd accept you. I don't want you any other way. I love the woman I've gotten to know—strong, independent and caring."

"What about my job?"

"I'm not going to kid you and say I'd be ecstatic to have you protecting others, putting your life on the line, but we can work something out. God didn't bring you into my life without a plan for us to be together. He'll never abandon me."

She took his face in her hands and kissed him. "We're two smart people. I think we can come up with a compromise."

EPILOGUE

In the early evening on Christmas eve, Elizabeth stood in the den near the decorated tree with Mary. "You've outdone yourself. I can't believe you threw this open house together in such a short time. The turnout has been great. I didn't know you all knew so many people."

"It's been a Caulder tradition for years. And this year, especially, we have something to celebrate. With Cindy in jail, my family is safe again and life is back to normal."

Elizabeth smiled. "As normal as it can be with a sixteen-year-old girl."

"True. I'm glad so many of her friends are here, too."

"And Brody." Elizabeth glanced toward the young man with Abbey. The night of the showdown with Cindy he'd only suffered a concussion like Slade. Otherwise, he had been all right and had been back at the ranch the next day, too.

"Poor Jake. I've invited him to share Christmas

dinner with us tomorrow. Him and Brody." Lifting her glass of red punch to her lips, Mary took a sip and looked around until she found Joshua. "Also your uncle."

"Yeah, he told me. Is there anything I should know about you two?"

"Who knows?" Mary murmured with a wink.

"Everyone, can I have your attention?" Slade stood in front of the fireplace, which was strung with garlands. When the room of guests quieted, Slade continued. "I have an announcement." Then he crossed to Elizabeth and tugged her toward the mantel.

A blush stained her cheeks at being the center of everyone's attention. "What's this about?"

Slade knelt on one knee, took hold of her hand and withdrew a ring from his pocket. "Elizabeth Walker, will you do me the honor of becoming my wife?"

The heat of her face rivaled the warmth from the blaze in the fireplace. She knew he loved her. She loved him, too—so much that she'd gone into the security consulting business with her uncle so she didn't have to travel much or put her life on the line for a client. But she hadn't expected this. Slade was a private man and to do this so publicly was out of character. "I—I don't know what to say" was all she could think to utter, she was so surprised by his proposal.

"'Yes' would be a good start."

"Yes. Yes."

Slade rose and slid the ring onto the third finger on her left hand.

"Kiss her," a female shouted. Elizabeth was pretty sure it was Abbey.

Someone else said the same thing, and in a few seconds the crowd was chanting it.

Slade pressed her against him, his arms wrapping around her. "We can't disappoint them."

"I agree."

He took her lips in a deep kiss that erased all past hurts. Only the future lay before them—together.

* * * * *

Dear Reader,

Christmas Bodyguard is the first in my series called Guardians, Inc. This series is about women who have chosen to be bodyguards. It has been interesting coming up with circumstances where the woman is the protector and then having the hero match her. In this series, the women and men are both equally strong characters who know how to deal with dangerous situations.

I love hearing from readers. You can contact me at margaretdaley@gmail.com or at P. O. Box 2074, Tulsa, OK 74101. You can also learn more about my books at www.margaretdaley.com. I have a quarterly newsletter that you can sign up for on my website, or you can enter my monthly drawings by signing my guest book on the website.

Best wishes,

Margaret Daley

QUESTIONS FOR DISCUSSION

1. Trust is important in a relationship. Elizabeth didn't know how to trust because of her past relationships with her father and Bryan. Has anyone caused you to distrust him/her? Why? How did you settle it?

2. Slade and Abbey were faced with someone wanting to hurt them. Have you ever been really scared? How did you deal with it?

3. Slade didn't think the Lord heard his prayers, especially when his wife died. Have you ever thought that? What did you do?

4. Slade dealt with his grief by throwing himself into work rather than turning to the Lord and his family. How have you dealt with grief in the past?

5. Abbey's relationship with her father is rocky. Part of that is because she is a teenager trying to become independent, but the other part is that she doesn't think he loves her like he used to because he pushed her away when Abbey's mother died. Do you or someone

you know have a similar relationship with a parent? How have you or that parent dealt with the situation?

6. Elizabeth couldn't forgive her father. She never felt loved or valued as a child. Her past ruled her life. Is there something that happened in your past that has done that to you? How can you get past that?

7. Abbey's life was in danger. This was hard for Slade to handle. When life seems impossible, what do you do? Who do you turn to for help?

8. Who did you think was after Abbey and Slade? Why?

9. The villain was motivated by revenge. How can we get past wanting to hurt someone we thought hurt us?

10. When Elizabeth's ex-husband left her, she was forced to start over. Have you ever needed a fresh start in life? Did it help you? If not, what did you do next to make your life better?

11. Elizabeth was verbally abused by her husband. She'd molded her life around her husband's

needs and demands. Have you ever been in a situation like that? What did you do to form a healthier relationship?

12. How would you deal with having your child kidnapped? Who would you turn to?

LARGER-PRINT BOOKS!

**GET 2 FREE
LARGER-PRINT NOVELS
PLUS 2 FREE
MYSTERY GIFTS**

Love Inspired.

SUSPENSE

RIVETING INSPIRATIONAL ROMANCE

Larger-print novels are now available...

LISUSLP10R

LARGER-PRINT BOOKS!

GET 2 FREE LARGER-PRINT NOVELS PLUS 2 FREE MYSTERY GIFTS

Larger-print novels are now available...

LILP10R